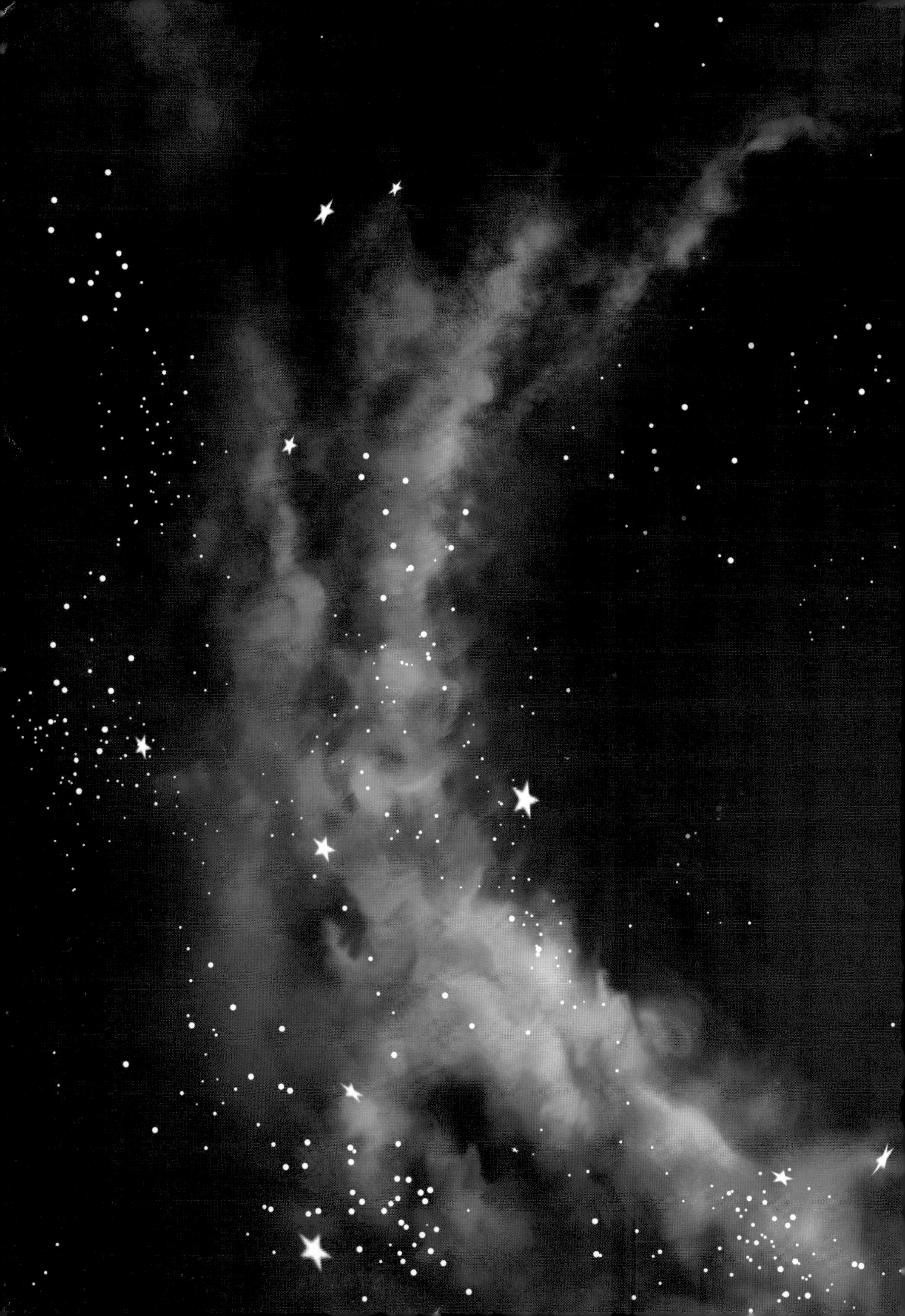

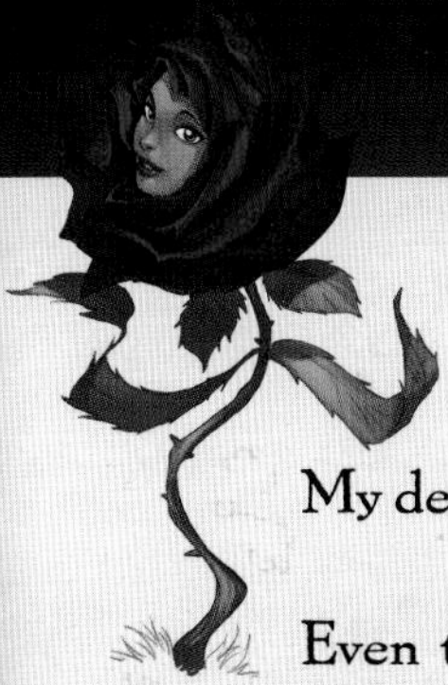

My dear Rose,

Even though it was under difficult circumstances, I'm so happy to have seen you on the planet of the Astronomer. Am I being selfish? Because of me, you were placed in danger. I realized that we never know how much we care about others until we're in danger of losing them. I don't know what I'd do without you and Fox. Deep in my heart, I know that the Snake will one day try to use my fear of losing you, just as he has done with the fears of all his victims. How will I react? How could I choose between the well-being of an entire planet and my friends? Is this what it's like to be a grown-up, having to make impossible choices? When I think about you, I hope that I'll always find the strength to stay on the right path.

Right now, a dark planet looms in our path...with a little spot of bright light.

Are the inhabitants fighting off the Snake's shadows?

The Little Prince

First American edition published in 2013 by Graphic Universe™.

Le Petit Prince™

based on the masterpiece by Antoine de Saint-Exupéry

© 2013 LPPM
An animated series based on the novel *Le Petit Prince* by Antoine de Saint-Exupéry
Developed for television by Matthieu Delaporte, Alexandre de la Patellière, and Bertrand Gatignol
Directed by Pierre-Alain Chartier

© 2013 ÉDITIONS GLÉNAT
Copyright © 2013 by Lerner Publishing Group, Inc., for the current edition

Graphic Universe™
A division of Lerner Publishing Group, Inc.
241 First Avenue North
Minneapolis, MN 55401 U.S.A.

Website address: www.lernerbooks.com

Library of Congress Cataloging-in-Publication Data

Gonnard, Christel.
   [Planète des Globus. English]
   The planet of the night globes / story by Christel Gonnard ; design and illustrations by Élyum Studio ; adaptation by Guillaume Dorison ; translation, Carol Klio Burrell. — 1st American ed.
     p. cm. — (The little prince ; #06)
   ISBN 978-0-7613-8756-5 (lib. bdg. : alk. paper)
   1. Graphic novels. I. Dorison, Guillaume. II. Burrell, Carol Klio. III. Saint-Exupéry, Antoine de, 1900-1944. Petit prince. IV. Élyum Studio. V. Petit Prince (Television program) VI. Title.
PZ7.7.G655Pl 2013
741.5'944—dc23   2012028621

Manufactured in the United States of America
1 — DP — 12/31/12

THE NEW ADVENTURES
BASED ON THE MASTERPIECE BY ANTOINE DE SAINT-EXUPÉRY

The Little Prince

THE PLANET OF THE NIGHT GLOBES

Based on the animated series and an original story by Christel Gonnard

Design: Élyum Studio
Story: Guillaume Dorison
Artistic Direction: Didier Poli
Art: Diane Fayolle
Backgrounds: Jérôme Benoit & Isa Python
Coloring: Karine Lambin
Coloring (Flats): Jackyung Kim
Editing: Hong Kim-Seang
Editorial Consultant: Didier Convard

Translation: Carol Burrell

Graphic Universe™ • Minneapolis • New York

THE LITTLE PRINCE

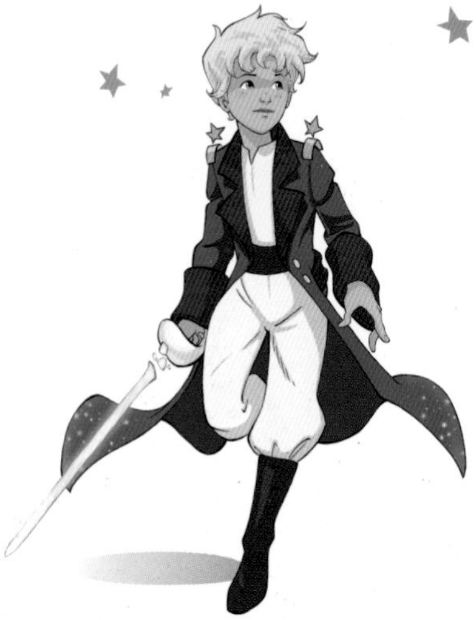

The Little Prince has extraordinary gifts. His sense of wonder allows him to discover what no one else can see. The Little Prince can communicate with all the beings in the universe, even the animals and plants. His powers grow over the course of his adventures.

The Prince's uniform:
When he transforms into the uniform of a prince, he is more agile and quick. When faced with difficult situations, the Little Prince also uses a sword that lets him sketch and bring to life anything from his imagination.

His sketchbook:
When he is not in his Prince's clothing, the Little Prince carries a sketchbook. When he blows on the pages, they take wing and form objects that he'll find very useful. Like his sword, it's powered by stardust collected on his travels.

FOX

A grouch, a trickster, and, so he says, interested only in his next meal, Fox is in reality the Little Prince's best friend. As such, he is always there to give him help but also just as much to help him to grow and to learn about the world.

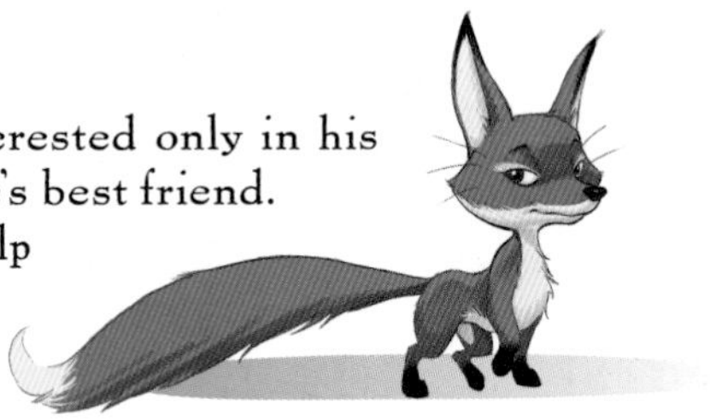

THE SNAKE

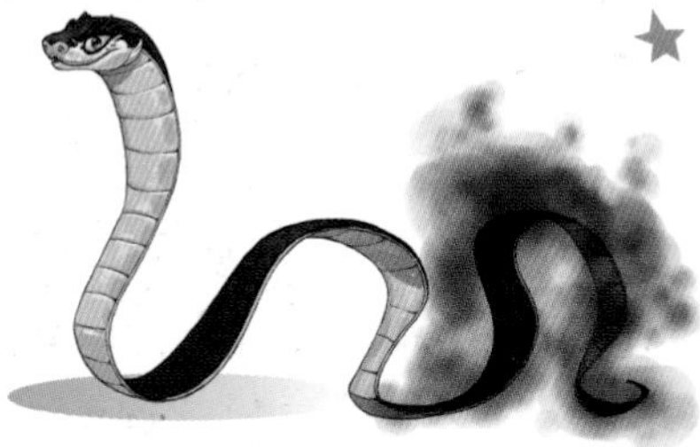

Even though the Little Prince still does not know exactly why, there can be no doubt that the Snake has set his mind to plunging the entire universe into darkness! And to accomplish his goal, this malicious being is ready to use any form of deception. However, the Snake never takes action himself. He prefers to bring out the wickedness in those beings he has chosen to bite, tempting them to put their own worlds in danger.

THE GLOOMIES

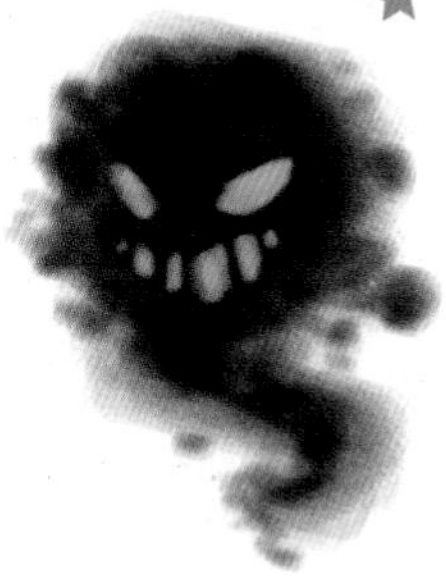

When people who have been "bitten" by the Snake have completely destroyed their own planets, they become Gloomies, slaves to their Snake master. The Gloomies act as a group and carry out the Snake's most vile orders so he can get the better of the Little Prince!

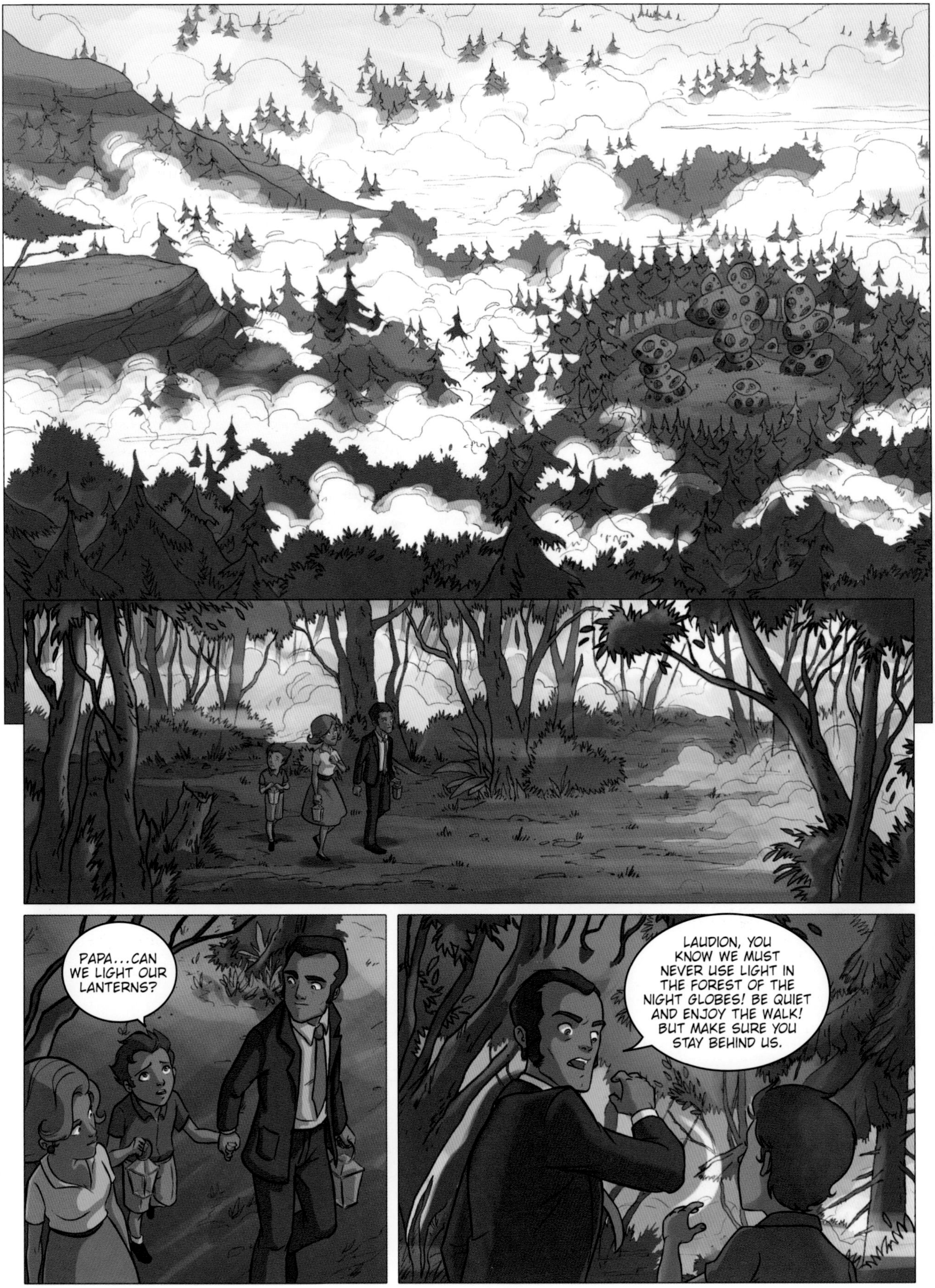
PAPA...CAN WE LIGHT OUR LANTERNS?
LAUDION, YOU KNOW WE MUST NEVER USE LIGHT IN THE FOREST OF THE NIGHT GLOBES! BE QUIET AND ENJOY THE WALK! BUT MAKE SURE YOU STAY BEHIND US.

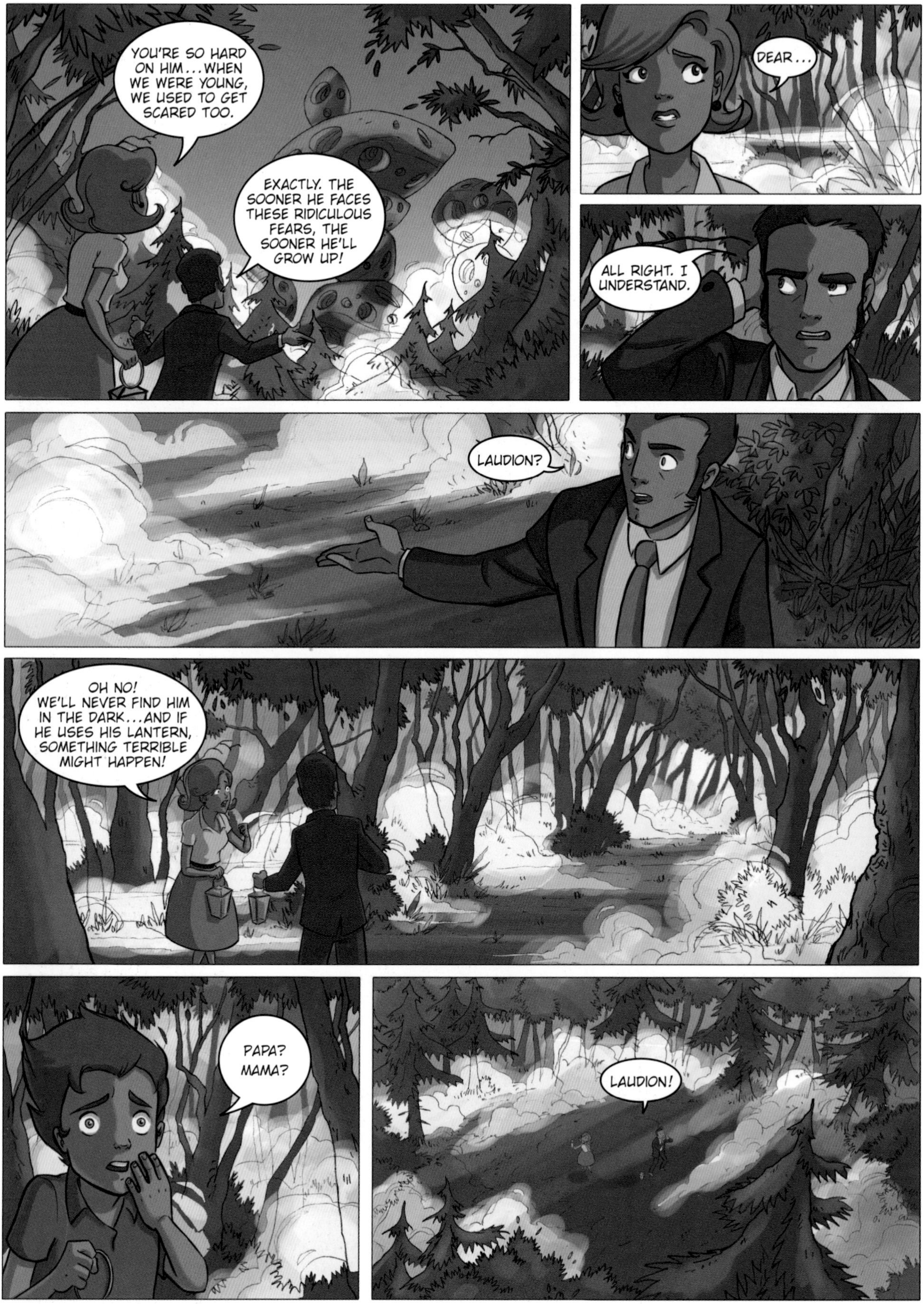
YOU'RE SO HARD ON HIM...WHEN WE WERE YOUNG, WE USED TO GET SCARED TOO.
EXACTLY. THE SOONER HE FACES THESE RIDICULOUS FEARS, THE SOONER HE'LL GROW UP!
DEAR...
ALL RIGHT. I UNDERSTAND.
LAUDION?
OH NO! WE'LL NEVER FIND HIM IN THE DARK...AND IF HE USES HIS LANTERN, SOMETHING TERRIBLE MIGHT HAPPEN!
PAPA? MAMA?
LAUDION!

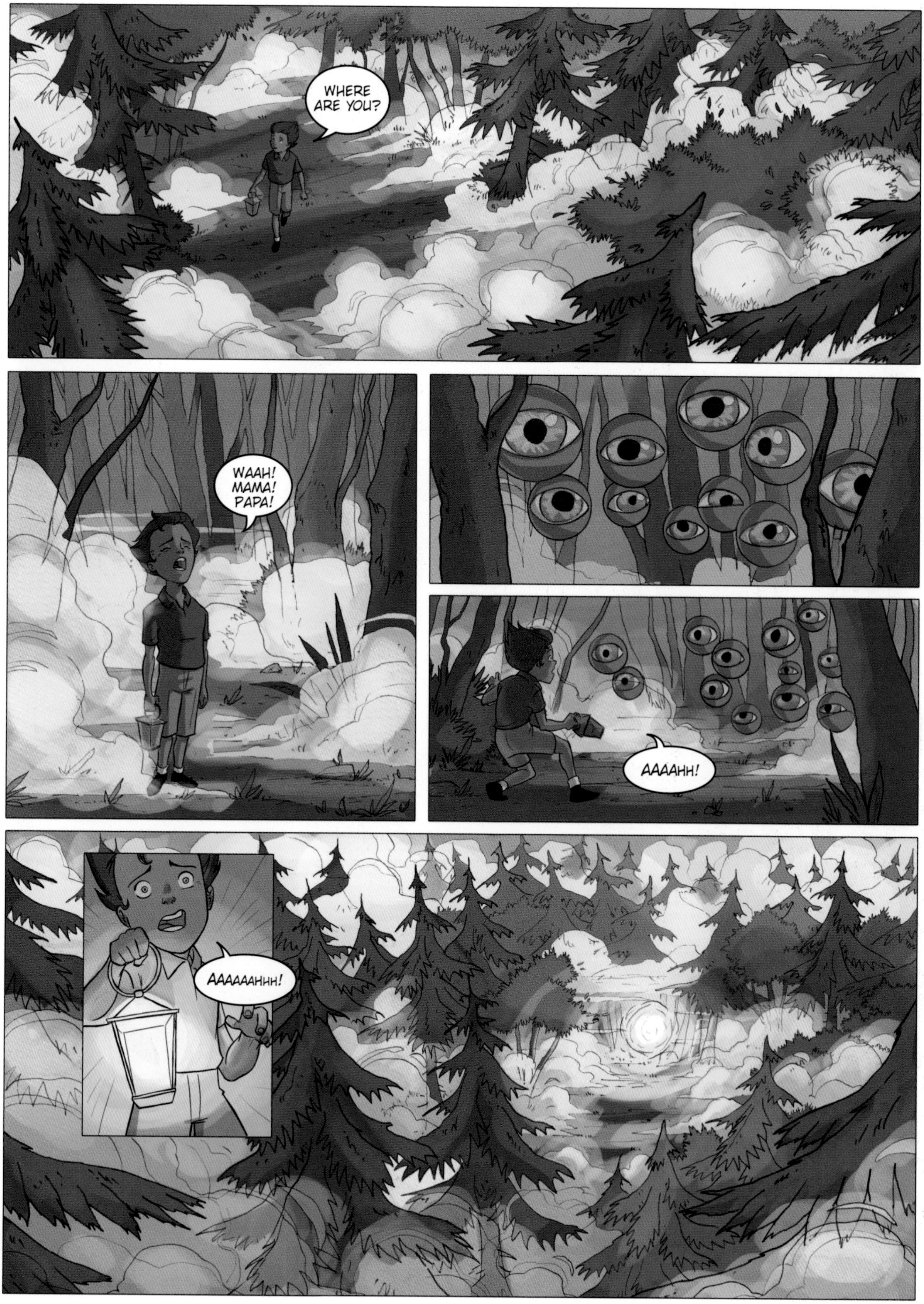
WHERE ARE YOU?
WAAH! MAMA! PAPA!
AAAAHH!
AAAAAAHHH!

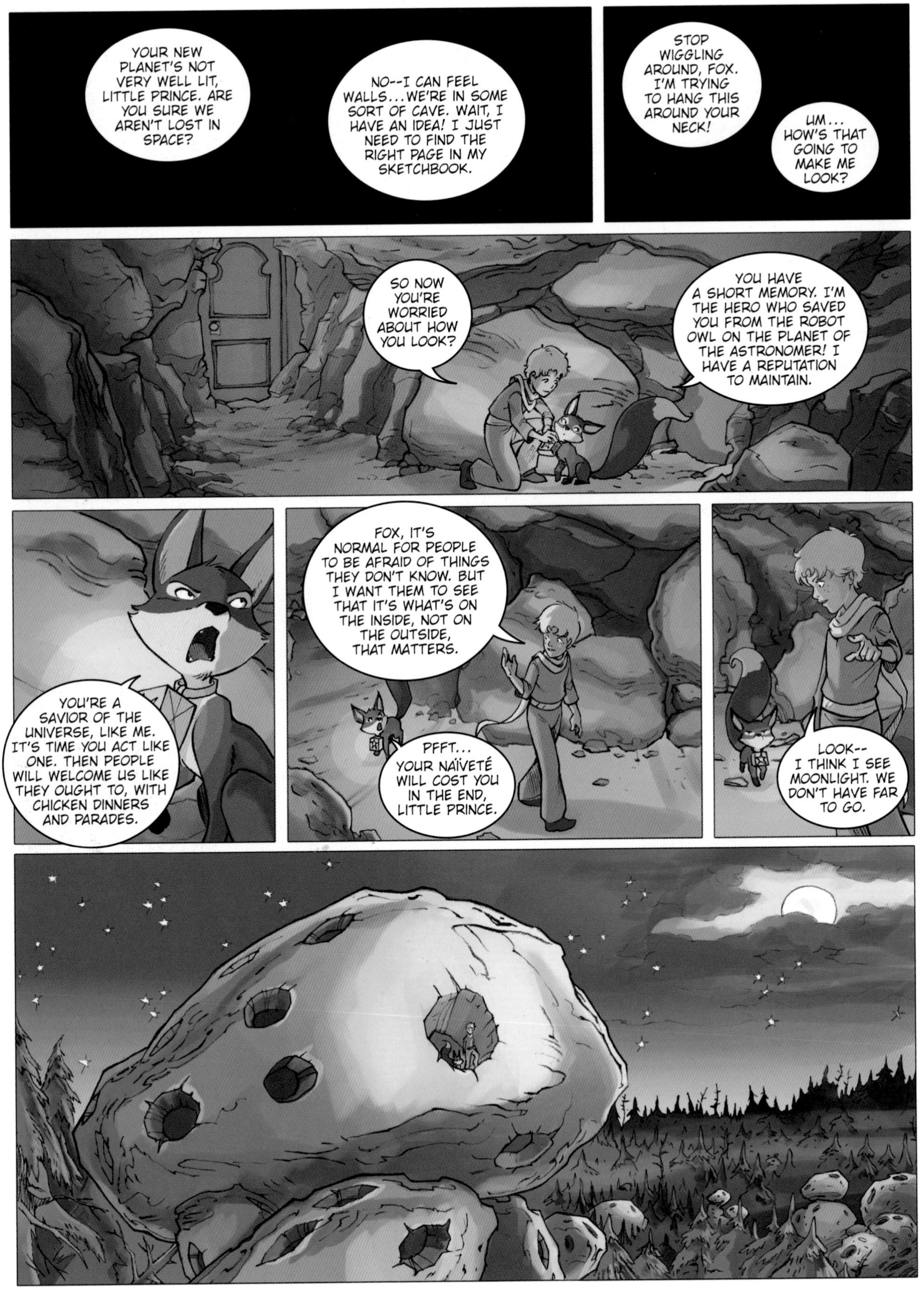

YOUR NEW PLANET'S NOT VERY WELL LIT, LITTLE PRINCE. ARE YOU SURE WE AREN'T LOST IN SPACE?
NO--I CAN FEEL WALLS...WE'RE IN SOME SORT OF CAVE. WAIT, I HAVE AN IDEA! I JUST NEED TO FIND THE RIGHT PAGE IN MY SKETCHBOOK.
STOP WIGGLING AROUND, FOX. I'M TRYING TO HANG THIS AROUND YOUR NECK!
UM... HOW'S THAT GOING TO MAKE ME LOOK?
SO NOW YOU'RE WORRIED ABOUT HOW YOU LOOK?
YOU HAVE A SHORT MEMORY. I'M THE HERO WHO SAVED YOU FROM THE ROBOT OWL ON THE PLANET OF THE ASTRONOMER! I HAVE A REPUTATION TO MAINTAIN.
YOU'RE A SAVIOR OF THE UNIVERSE, LIKE ME. IT'S TIME YOU ACT LIKE ONE. THEN PEOPLE WILL WELCOME US LIKE THEY OUGHT TO, WITH CHICKEN DINNERS AND PARADES.
FOX, IT'S NORMAL FOR PEOPLE TO BE AFRAID OF THINGS THEY DON'T KNOW. BUT I WANT THEM TO SEE THAT IT'S WHAT'S ON THE INSIDE, NOT ON THE OUTSIDE, THAT MATTERS.
PFFT... YOUR NAÏVETÉ WILL COST YOU IN THE END, LITTLE PRINCE.
LOOK-- I THINK I SEE MOONLIGHT. WE DON'T HAVE FAR TO GO.

NO CHOICE... WE'LL HAVE TO CLIMB DOWN!

THIS PLACE ISN'T VERY REASSURING.

WELL, IT'S TRUE THAT IN THE DARK, NO ONE CAN SEE YOUR NEW CHARISMA. HA HA HA!

HMM... I THINK THERE'S SOMETHING IN THOSE ROCKS. GIVE ME SOME LIGHT, FOX.

HUFF PUFF ARF...

WUFF-- ARRGH!

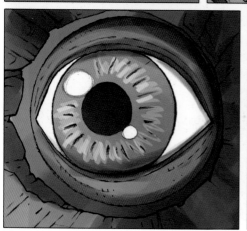

AAAHHH!

7

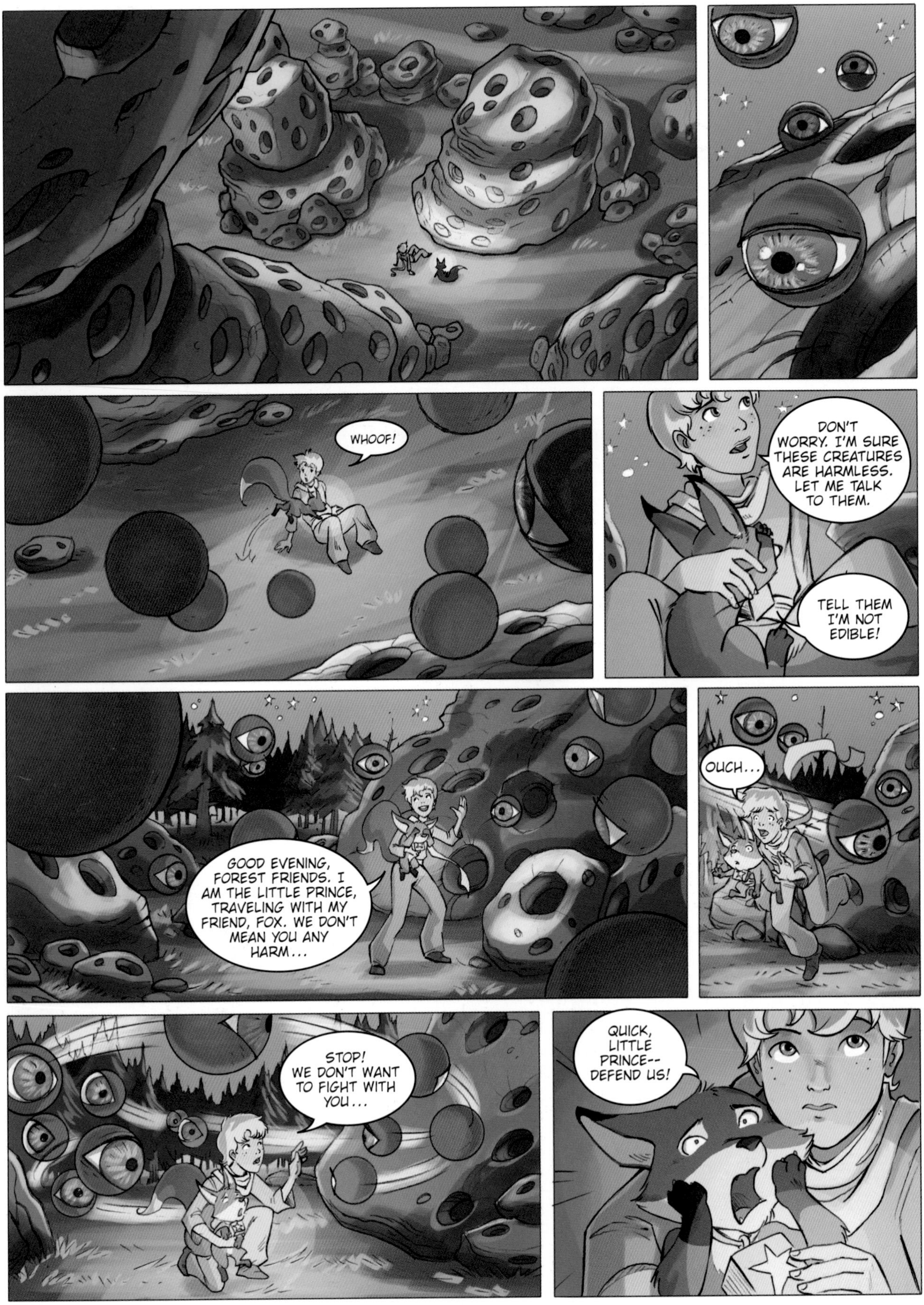
WHOOF!
DON'T WORRY. I'M SURE THESE CREATURES ARE HARMLESS. LET ME TALK TO THEM.
TELL THEM I'M NOT EDIBLE!
GOOD EVENING, FOREST FRIENDS. I AM THE LITTLE PRINCE, TRAVELING WITH MY FRIEND, FOX. WE DON'T MEAN YOU ANY HARM...
OUCH...
STOP! WE DON'T WANT TO FIGHT WITH YOU...
QUICK, LITTLE PRINCE-- DEFEND US!

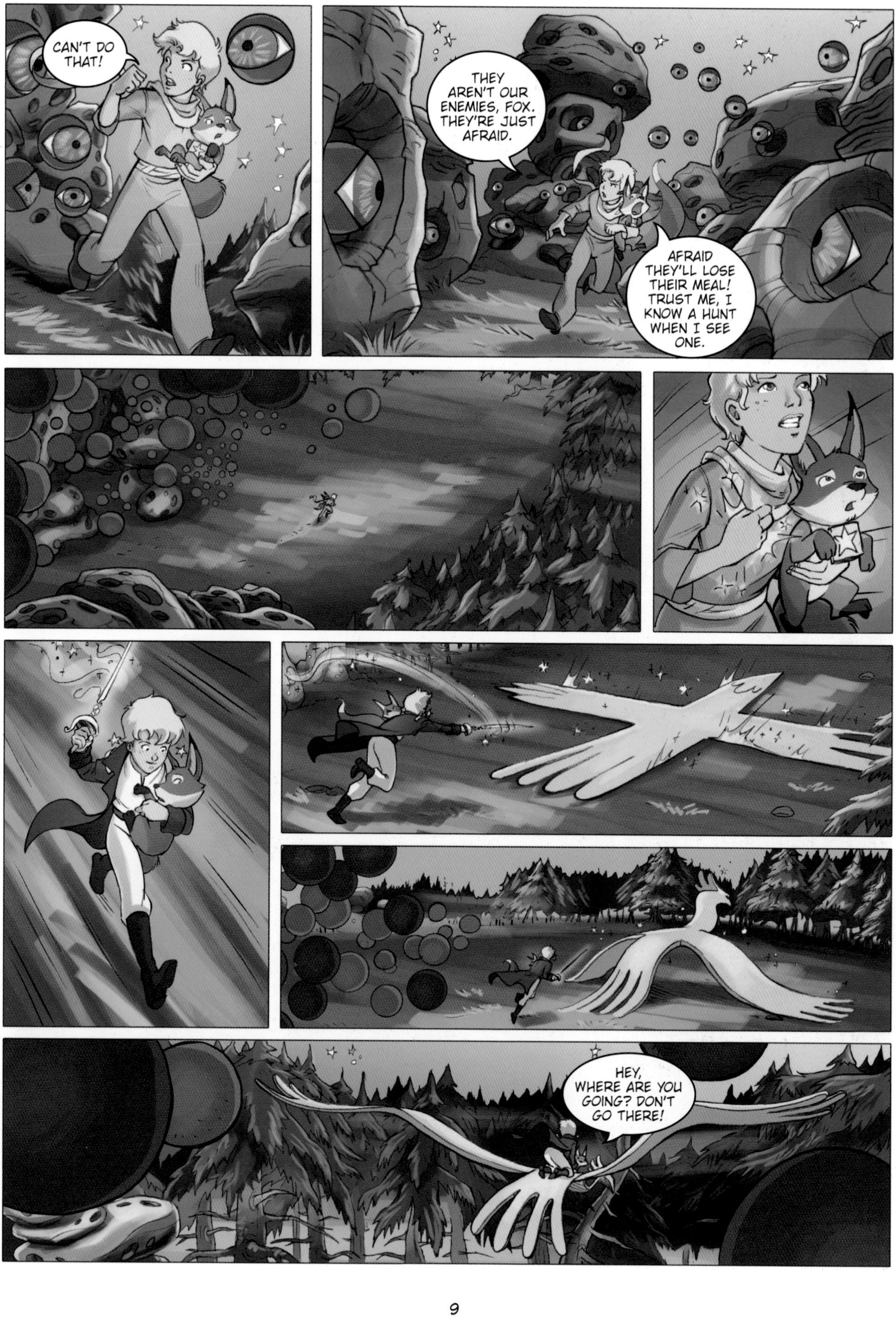
CAN'T DO THAT!
THEY AREN'T OUR ENEMIES, FOX. THEY'RE JUST AFRAID.
AFRAID THEY'LL LOSE THEIR MEAL! TRUST ME, I KNOW A HUNT WHEN I SEE ONE.
HEY, WHERE ARE YOU GOING? DON'T GO THERE!

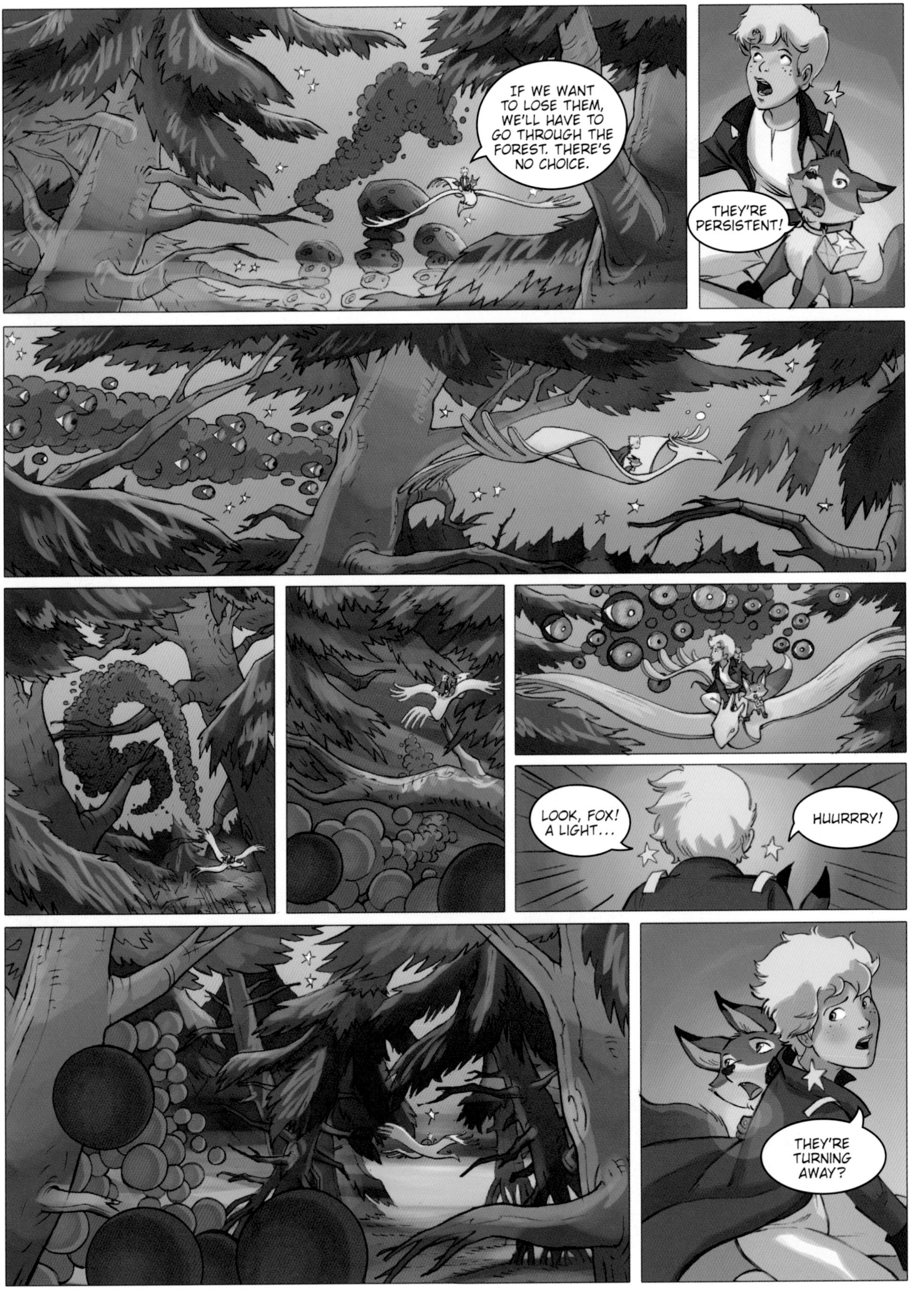
IF WE WANT TO LOSE THEM, WE'LL HAVE TO GO THROUGH THE FOREST. THERE'S NO CHOICE.
THEY'RE PERSISTENT!
LOOK, FOX! A LIGHT...
HUURRRY!
THEY'RE TURNING AWAY?

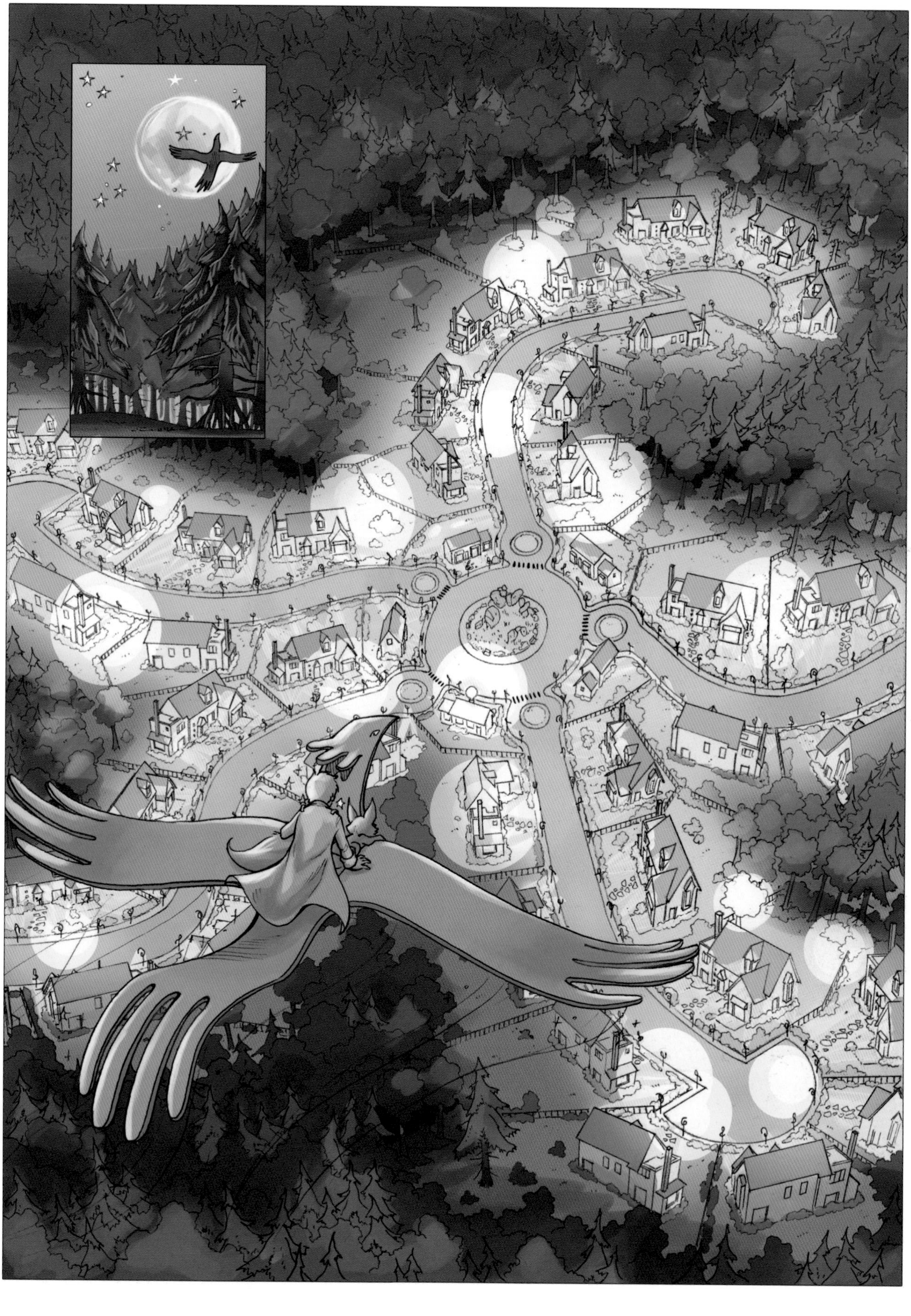

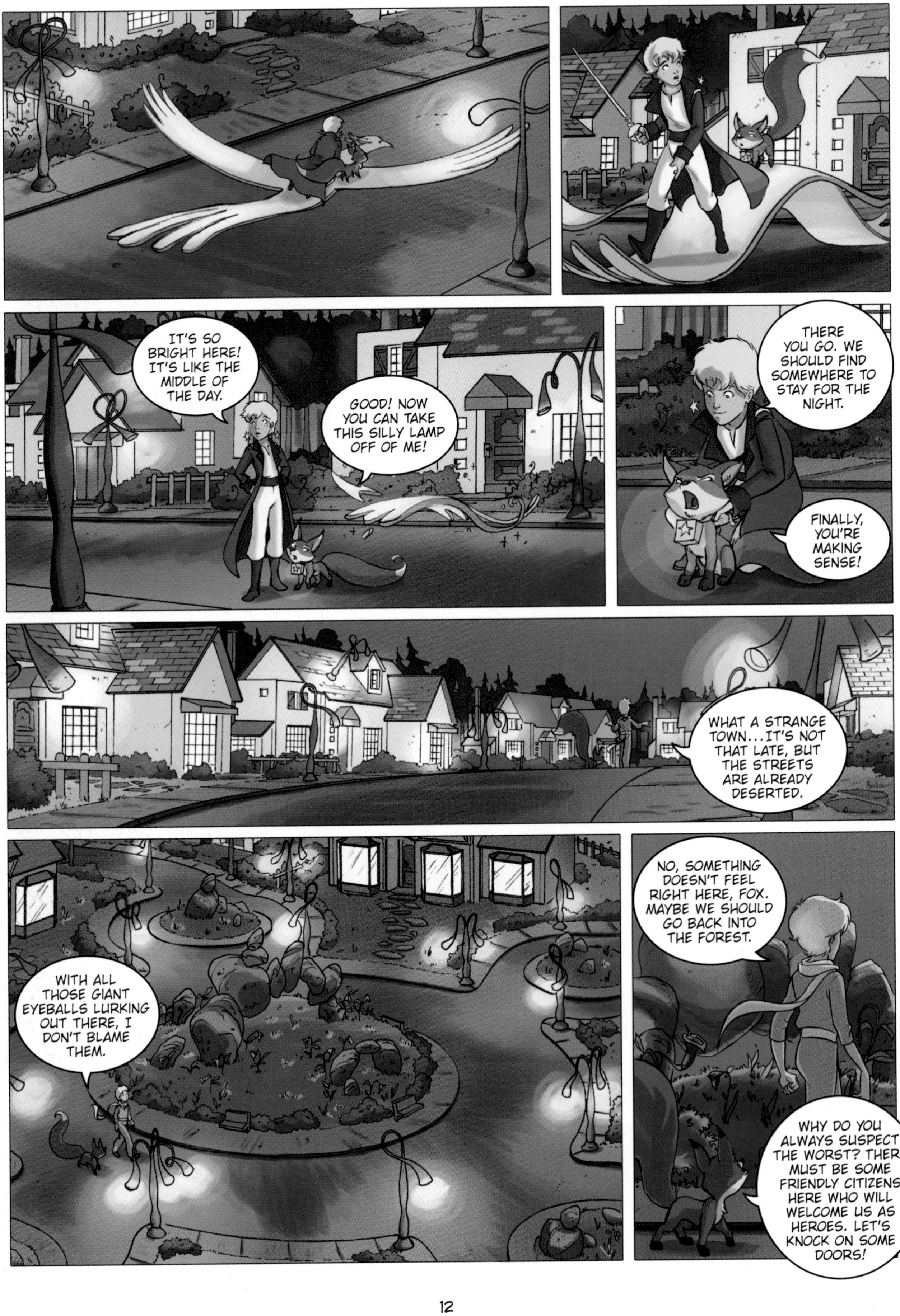
IT'S SO BRIGHT HERE! IT'S LIKE THE MIDDLE OF THE DAY.
GOOD! NOW YOU CAN TAKE THIS SILLY LAMP OFF OF ME!
THERE YOU GO. WE SHOULD FIND SOMEWHERE TO STAY FOR THE NIGHT.
FINALLY, YOU'RE MAKING SENSE!
WHAT A STRANGE TOWN... IT'S NOT THAT LATE, BUT THE STREETS ARE ALREADY DESERTED.
WITH ALL THOSE GIANT EYEBALLS LURKING OUT THERE, I DON'T BLAME THEM.
NO, SOMETHING DOESN'T FEEL RIGHT HERE, FOX. MAYBE WE SHOULD GO BACK INTO THE FOREST.
WHY DO YOU ALWAYS SUSPECT THE WORST? THERE MUST BE SOME FRIENDLY CITIZENS HERE WHO WILL WELCOME US AS HEROES. LET'S KNOCK ON SOME DOORS!

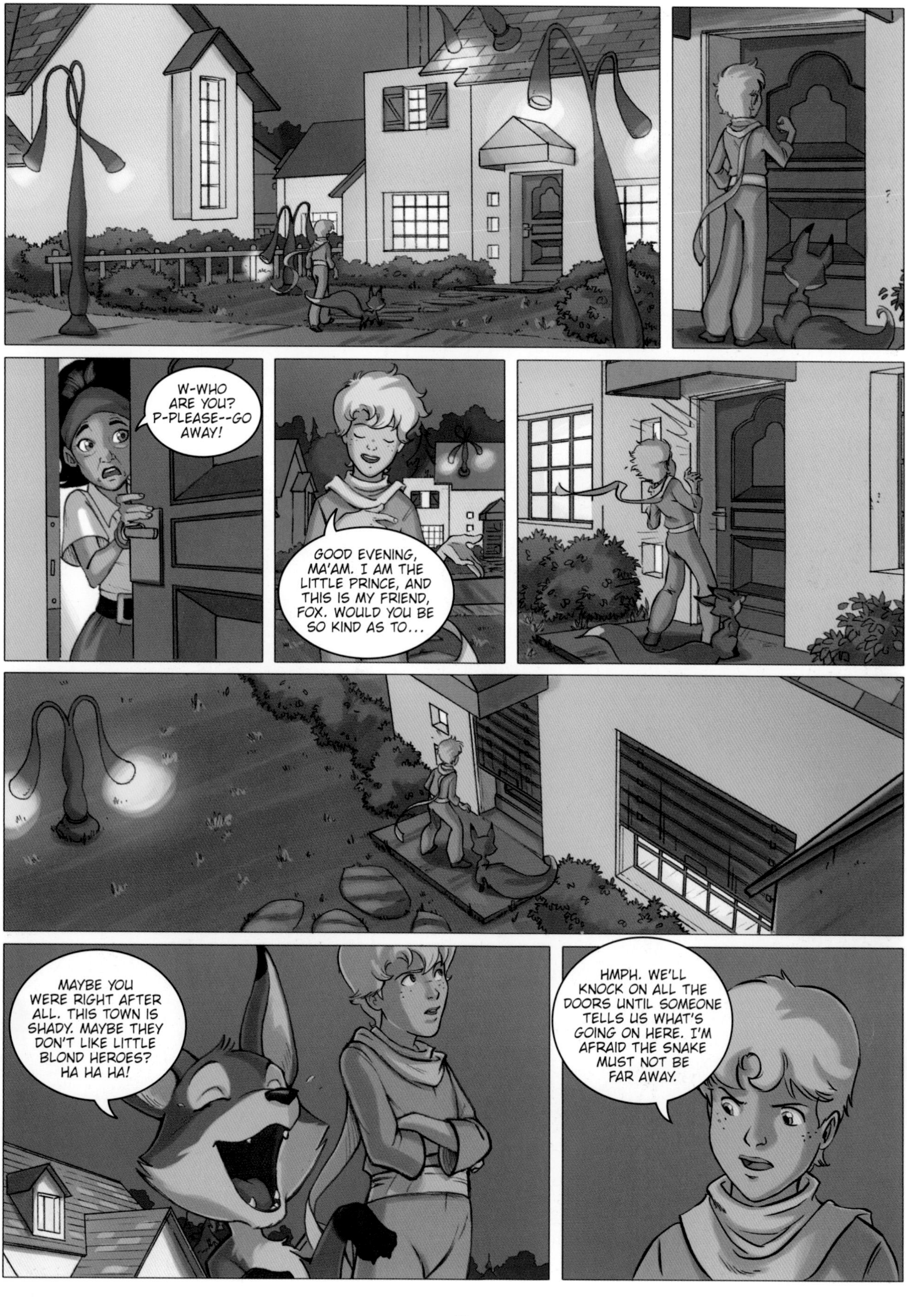
W-WHO ARE YOU? P-PLEASE--GO AWAY!
GOOD EVENING, MA'AM. I AM THE LITTLE PRINCE, AND THIS IS MY FRIEND, FOX. WOULD YOU BE SO KIND AS TO...
MAYBE YOU WERE RIGHT AFTER ALL. THIS TOWN IS SHADY. MAYBE THEY DON'T LIKE LITTLE BLOND HEROES? HA HA HA!
HMPH. WE'LL KNOCK ON ALL THE DOORS UNTIL SOMEONE TELLS US WHAT'S GOING ON HERE. I'M AFRAID THE SNAKE MUST NOT BE FAR AWAY.

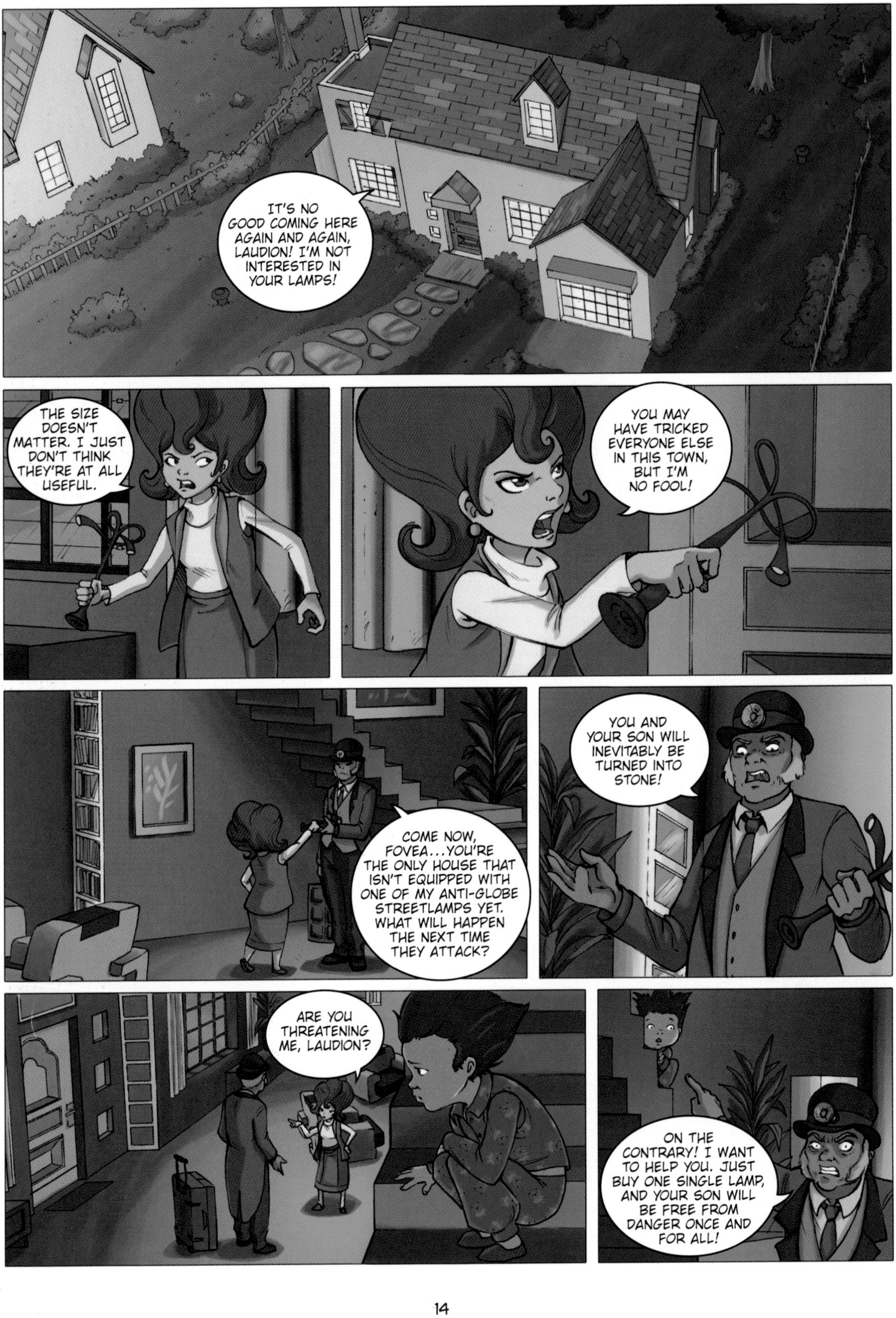
IT'S NO GOOD COMING HERE AGAIN AND AGAIN, LAUDION! I'M NOT INTERESTED IN YOUR LAMPS!
THE SIZE DOESN'T MATTER. I JUST DON'T THINK THEY'RE AT ALL USEFUL.
YOU MAY HAVE TRICKED EVERYONE ELSE IN THIS TOWN, BUT I'M NO FOOL!
COME NOW, FOVEA...YOU'RE THE ONLY HOUSE THAT ISN'T EQUIPPED WITH ONE OF MY ANTI-GLOBE STREETLAMPS YET. WHAT WILL HAPPEN THE NEXT TIME THEY ATTACK?
YOU AND YOUR SON WILL INEVITABLY BE TURNED INTO STONE!
ARE YOU THREATENING ME, LAUDION?
ON THE CONTRARY! I WANT TO HELP YOU. JUST BUY ONE SINGLE LAMP, AND YOUR SON WILL BE FREE FROM DANGER ONCE AND FOR ALL!

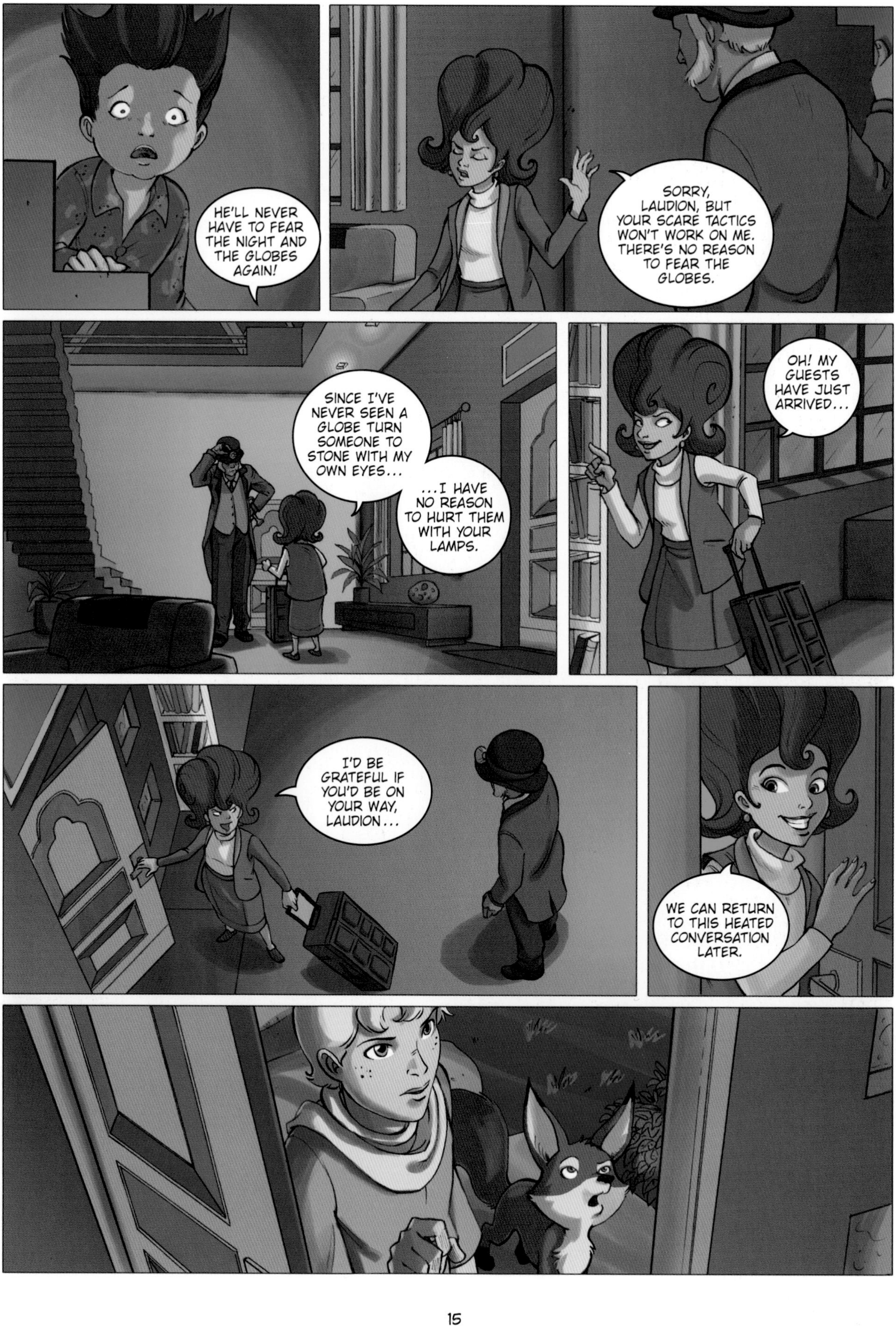
HE'LL NEVER HAVE TO FEAR THE NIGHT AND THE GLOBES AGAIN!
SORRY, LAUDION, BUT YOUR SCARE TACTICS WON'T WORK ON ME. THERE'S NO REASON TO FEAR THE GLOBES.
SINCE I'VE NEVER SEEN A GLOBE TURN SOMEONE TO STONE WITH MY OWN EYES...
...I HAVE NO REASON TO HURT THEM WITH YOUR LAMPS.
OH! MY GUESTS HAVE JUST ARRIVED...
I'D BE GRATEFUL IF YOU'D BE ON YOUR WAY, LAUDION...
WE CAN RETURN TO THIS HEATED CONVERSATION LATER.

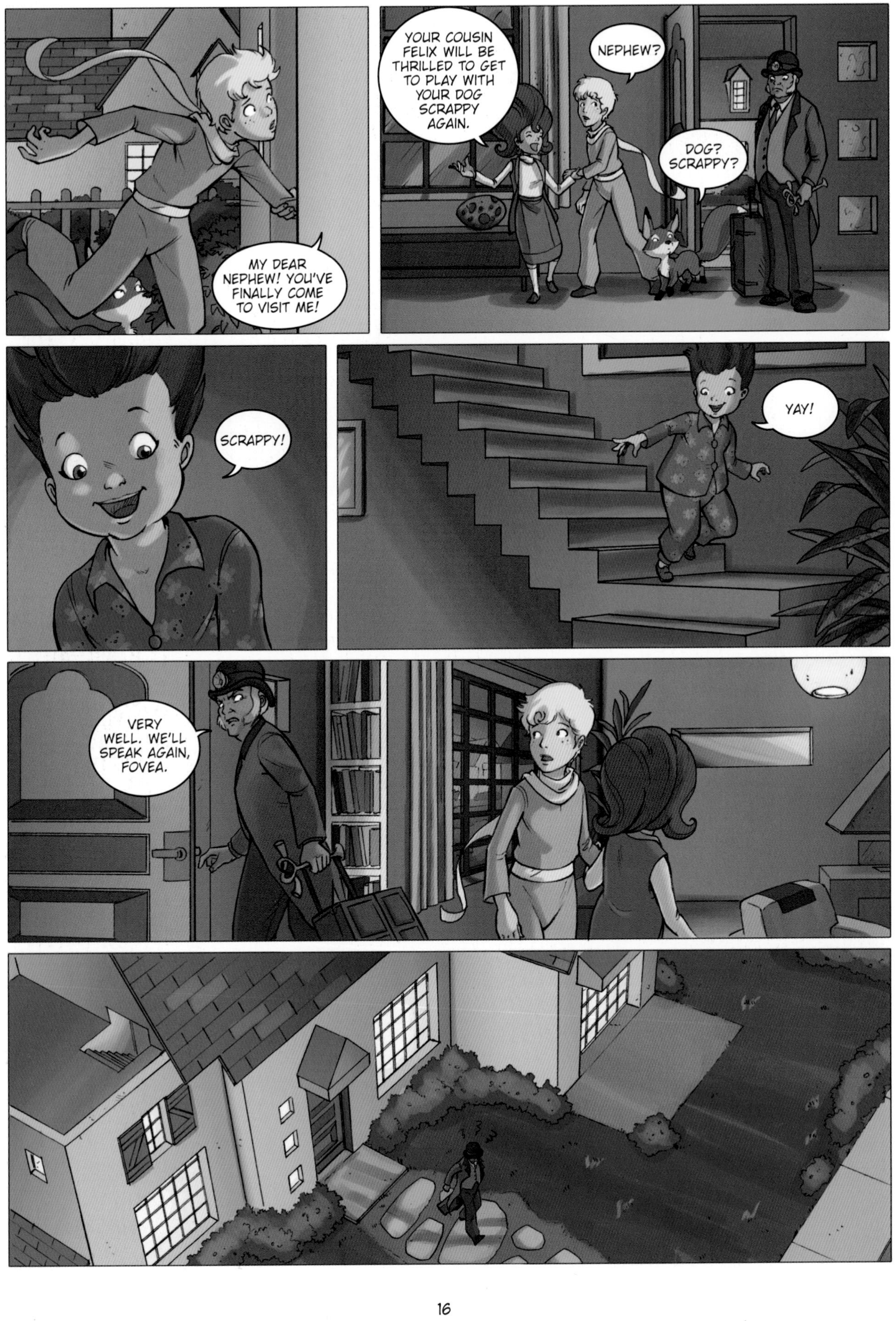
MY DEAR NEPHEW! YOU'VE FINALLY COME TO VISIT ME!
YOUR COUSIN FELIX WILL BE THRILLED TO GET TO PLAY WITH YOUR DOG SCRAPPY AGAIN.
NEPHEW?
DOG? SCRAPPY?
SCRAPPY!
YAY!
VERY WELL. WE'LL SPEAK AGAIN, FOVEA.

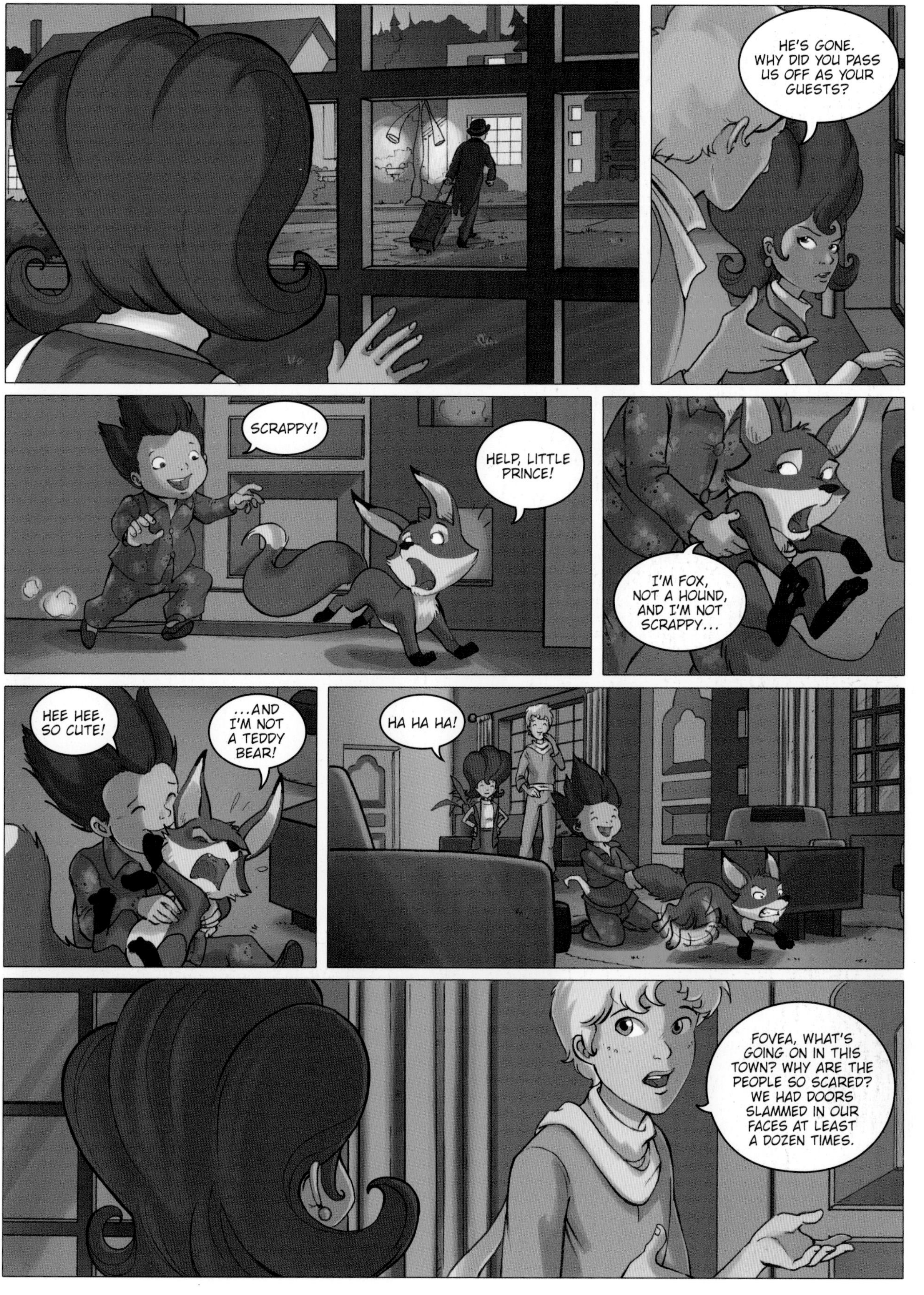
HE'S GONE. WHY DID YOU PASS US OFF AS YOUR GUESTS?
SCRAPPY!
HELP, LITTLE PRINCE!
I'M FOX, NOT A HOUND, AND I'M NOT SCRAPPY...
HEE HEE. SO CUTE!
...AND I'M NOT A TEDDY BEAR!
HA HA HA!
FOVEA, WHAT'S GOING ON IN THIS TOWN? WHY ARE THE PEOPLE SO SCARED? WE HAD DOORS SLAMMED IN OUR FACES AT LEAST A DOZEN TIMES.

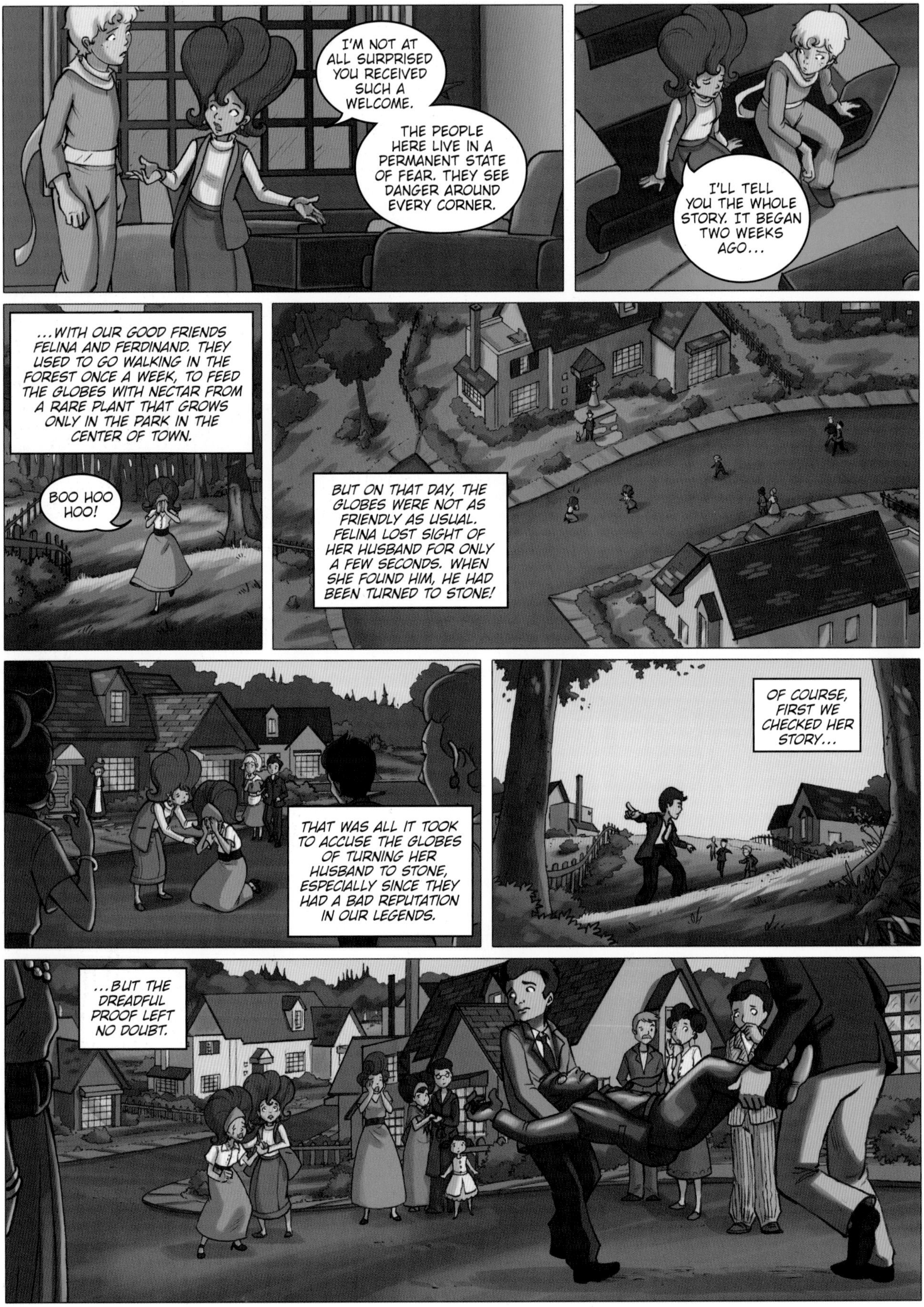
I'M NOT AT ALL SURPRISED YOU RECEIVED SUCH A WELCOME.
THE PEOPLE HERE LIVE IN A PERMANENT STATE OF FEAR. THEY SEE DANGER AROUND EVERY CORNER.
I'LL TELL YOU THE WHOLE STORY. IT BEGAN TWO WEEKS AGO...
...WITH OUR GOOD FRIENDS FELINA AND FERDINAND. THEY USED TO GO WALKING IN THE FOREST ONCE A WEEK, TO FEED THE GLOBES WITH NECTAR FROM A RARE PLANT THAT GROWS ONLY IN THE PARK IN THE CENTER OF TOWN.
BOO HOO HOO!
BUT ON THAT DAY, THE GLOBES WERE NOT AS FRIENDLY AS USUAL. FELINA LOST SIGHT OF HER HUSBAND FOR ONLY A FEW SECONDS. WHEN SHE FOUND HIM, HE HAD BEEN TURNED TO STONE!
THAT WAS ALL IT TOOK TO ACCUSE THE GLOBES OF TURNING HER HUSBAND TO STONE, ESPECIALLY SINCE THEY HAD A BAD REPUTATION IN OUR LEGENDS.
OF COURSE, FIRST WE CHECKED HER STORY...
...BUT THE DREADFUL PROOF LEFT NO DOUBT.

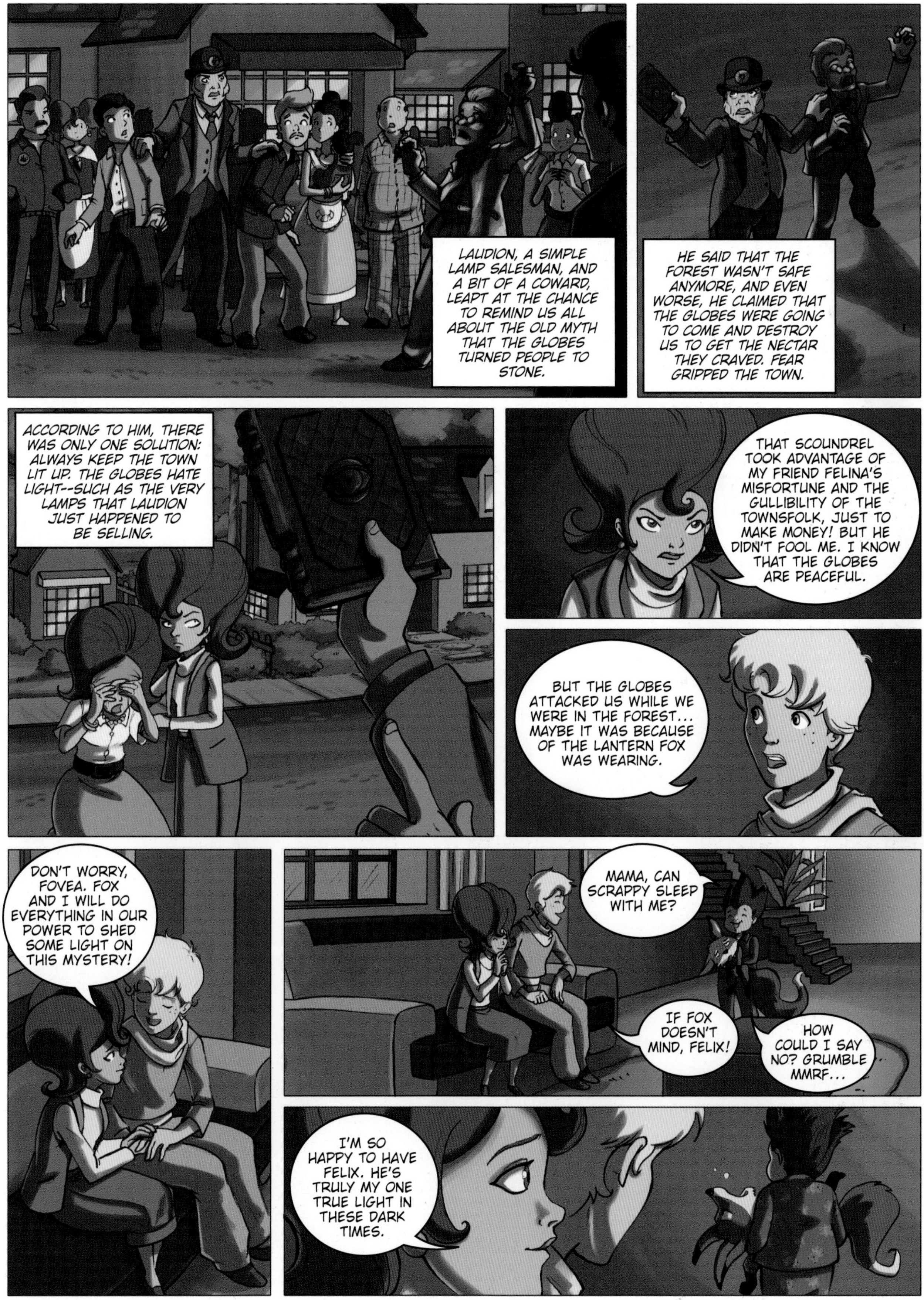

LAUDION, A SIMPLE LAMP SALESMAN, AND A BIT OF A COWARD, LEAPT AT THE CHANCE TO REMIND US ALL ABOUT THE OLD MYTH THAT THE GLOBES TURNED PEOPLE TO STONE.
HE SAID THAT THE FOREST WASN'T SAFE ANYMORE, AND EVEN WORSE, HE CLAIMED THAT THE GLOBES WERE GOING TO COME AND DESTROY US TO GET THE NECTAR THEY CRAVED. FEAR GRIPPED THE TOWN.
ACCORDING TO HIM, THERE WAS ONLY ONE SOLUTION: ALWAYS KEEP THE TOWN LIT UP. THE GLOBES HATE LIGHT--SUCH AS THE VERY LAMPS THAT LAUDION JUST HAPPENED TO BE SELLING.
THAT SCOUNDREL TOOK ADVANTAGE OF MY FRIEND FELINA'S MISFORTUNE AND THE GULLIBILITY OF THE TOWNSFOLK, JUST TO MAKE MONEY! BUT HE DIDN'T FOOL ME. I KNOW THAT THE GLOBES ARE PEACEFUL.
BUT THE GLOBES ATTACKED US WHILE WE WERE IN THE FOREST... MAYBE IT WAS BECAUSE OF THE LANTERN FOX WAS WEARING.
DON'T WORRY, FOVEA. FOX AND I WILL DO EVERYTHING IN OUR POWER TO SHED SOME LIGHT ON THIS MYSTERY!
MAMA, CAN SCRAPPY SLEEP WITH ME?
IF FOX DOESN'T MIND, FELIX!
HOW COULD I SAY NO? GRUMBLE MMRF...
I'M SO HAPPY TO HAVE FELIX. HE'S TRULY MY ONE TRUE LIGHT IN THESE DARK TIMES.

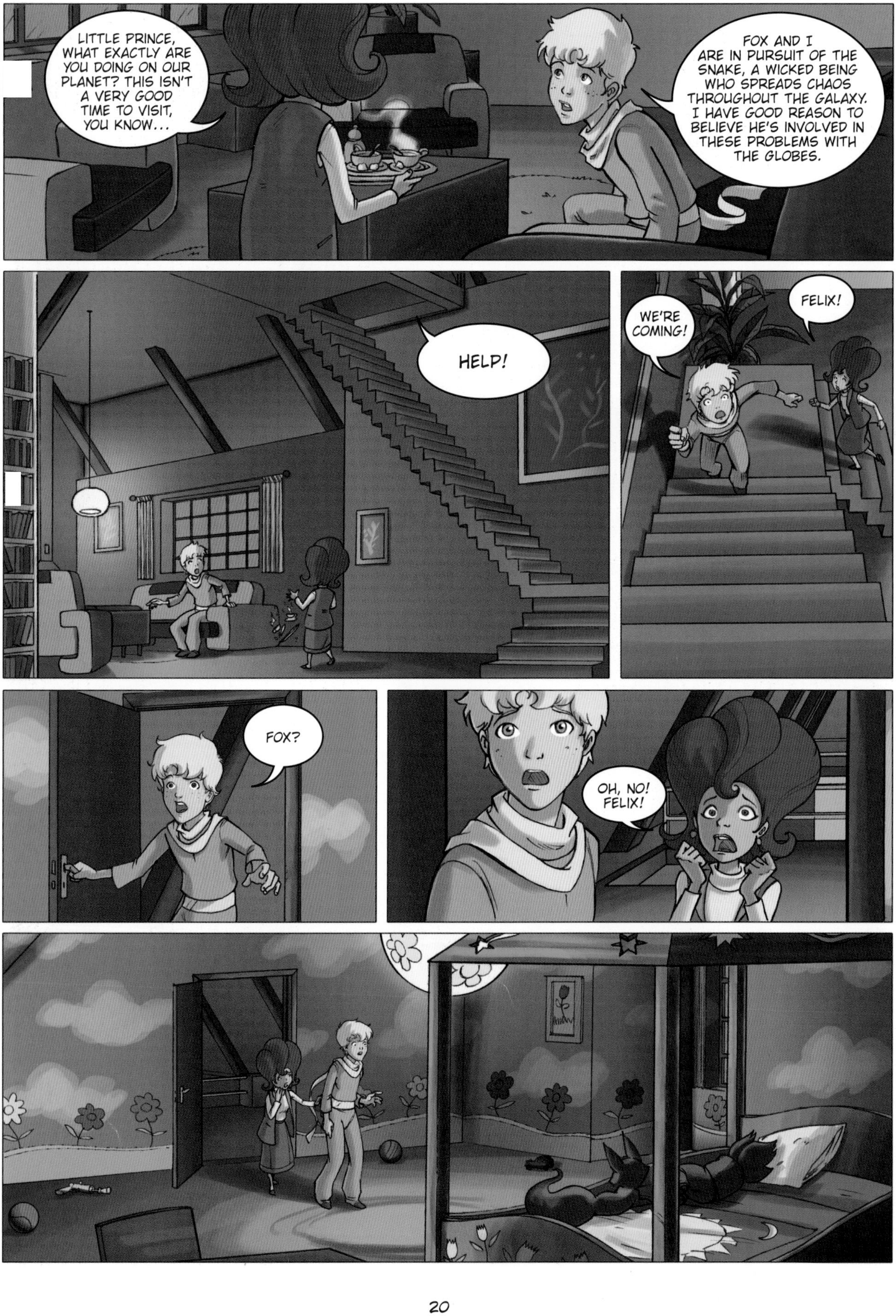
LITTLE PRINCE, WHAT EXACTLY ARE YOU DOING ON OUR PLANET? THIS ISN'T A VERY GOOD TIME TO VISIT, YOU KNOW...
FOX AND I ARE IN PURSUIT OF THE SNAKE, A WICKED BEING WHO SPREADS CHAOS THROUGHOUT THE GALAXY. I HAVE GOOD REASON TO BELIEVE HE'S INVOLVED IN THESE PROBLEMS WITH THE GLOBES.
HELP!
WE'RE COMING!
FELIX!
FOX?
OH, NO! FELIX!

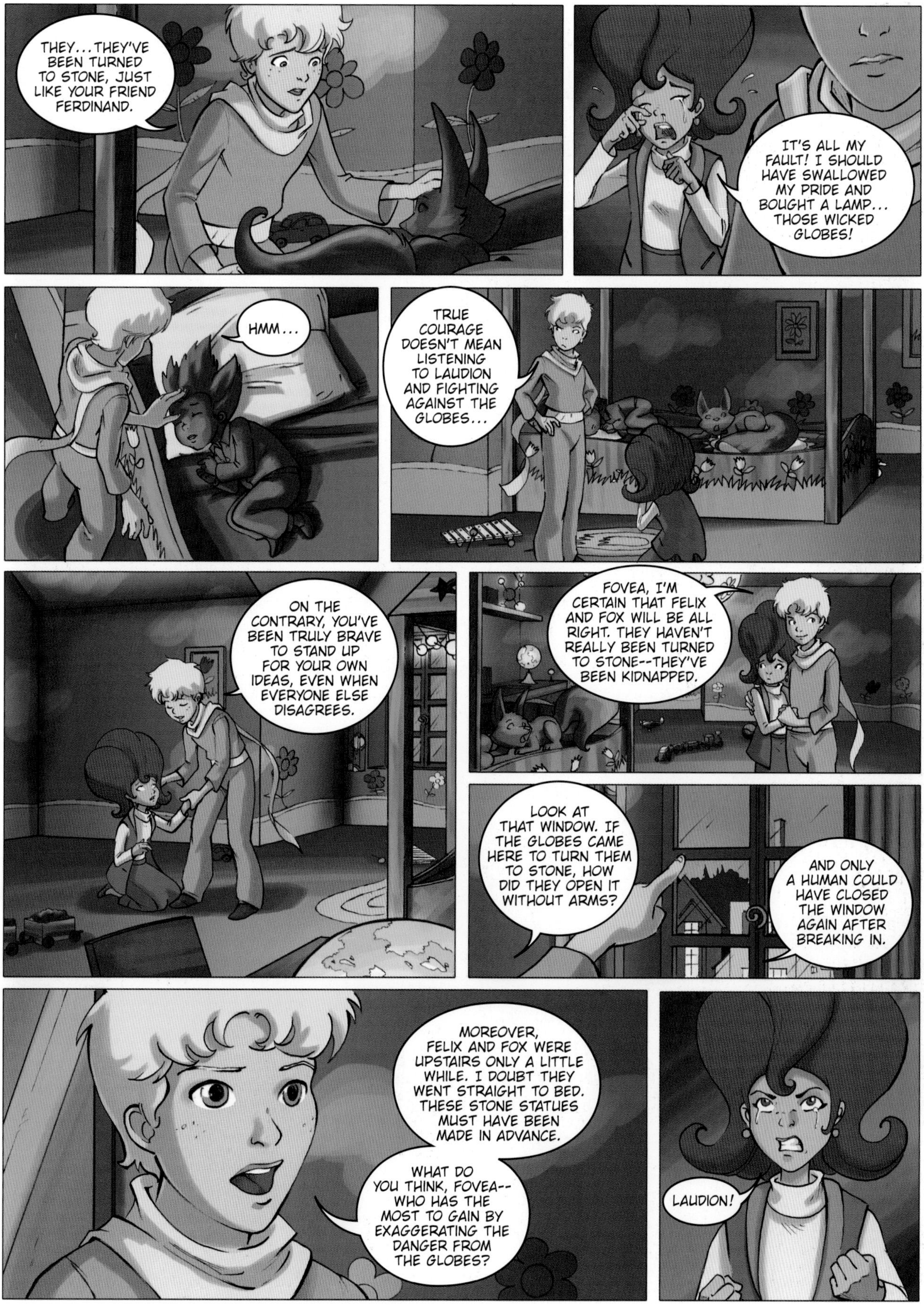
THEY... THEY'VE BEEN TURNED TO STONE, JUST LIKE YOUR FRIEND FERDINAND.
IT'S ALL MY FAULT! I SHOULD HAVE SWALLOWED MY PRIDE AND BOUGHT A LAMP... THOSE WICKED GLOBES!
HMM...
TRUE COURAGE DOESN'T MEAN LISTENING TO LAUDION AND FIGHTING AGAINST THE GLOBES...
ON THE CONTRARY, YOU'VE BEEN TRULY BRAVE TO STAND UP FOR YOUR OWN IDEAS, EVEN WHEN EVERYONE ELSE DISAGREES.
FOVEA, I'M CERTAIN THAT FELIX AND FOX WILL BE ALL RIGHT. THEY HAVEN'T REALLY BEEN TURNED TO STONE--THEY'VE BEEN KIDNAPPED.
LOOK AT THAT WINDOW. IF THE GLOBES CAME HERE TO TURN THEM TO STONE, HOW DID THEY OPEN IT WITHOUT ARMS?
AND ONLY A HUMAN COULD HAVE CLOSED THE WINDOW AGAIN AFTER BREAKING IN.
MOREOVER, FELIX AND FOX WERE UPSTAIRS ONLY A LITTLE WHILE. I DOUBT THEY WENT STRAIGHT TO BED. THESE STONE STATUES MUST HAVE BEEN MADE IN ADVANCE.
WHAT DO YOU THINK, FOVEA--WHO HAS THE MOST TO GAIN BY EXAGGERATING THE DANGER FROM THE GLOBES?
LAUDION!

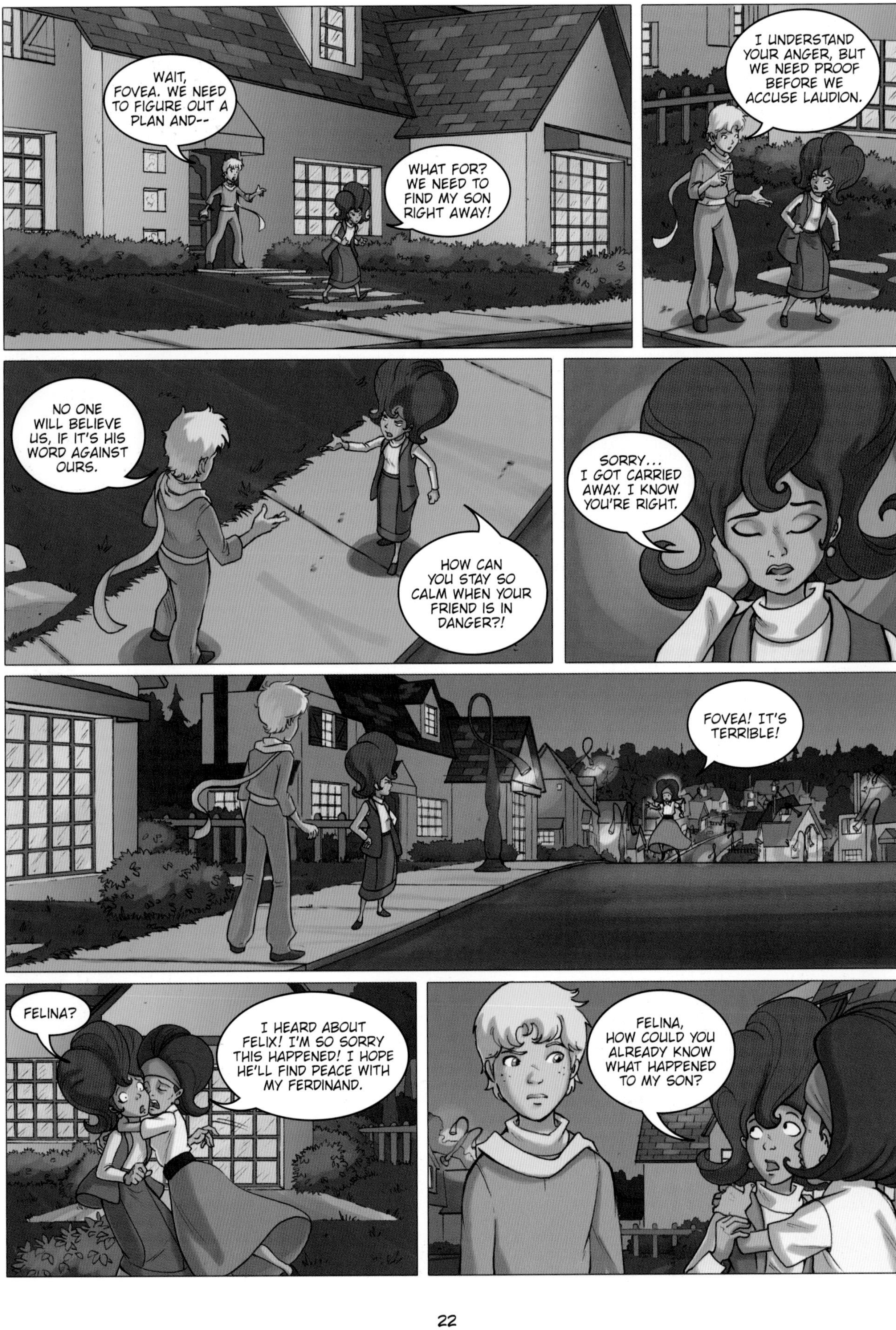
WAIT, FOVEA. WE NEED TO FIGURE OUT A PLAN AND--
WHAT FOR? WE NEED TO FIND MY SON RIGHT AWAY!
I UNDERSTAND YOUR ANGER, BUT WE NEED PROOF BEFORE WE ACCUSE LAUDION.
NO ONE WILL BELIEVE US, IF IT'S HIS WORD AGAINST OURS.
HOW CAN YOU STAY SO CALM WHEN YOUR FRIEND IS IN DANGER?!
SORRY... I GOT CARRIED AWAY. I KNOW YOU'RE RIGHT.
FOVEA! IT'S TERRIBLE!
FELINA?
I HEARD ABOUT FELIX! I'M SO SORRY THIS HAPPENED! I HOPE HE'LL FIND PEACE WITH MY FERDINAND.
FELINA, HOW COULD YOU ALREADY KNOW WHAT HAPPENED TO MY SON?

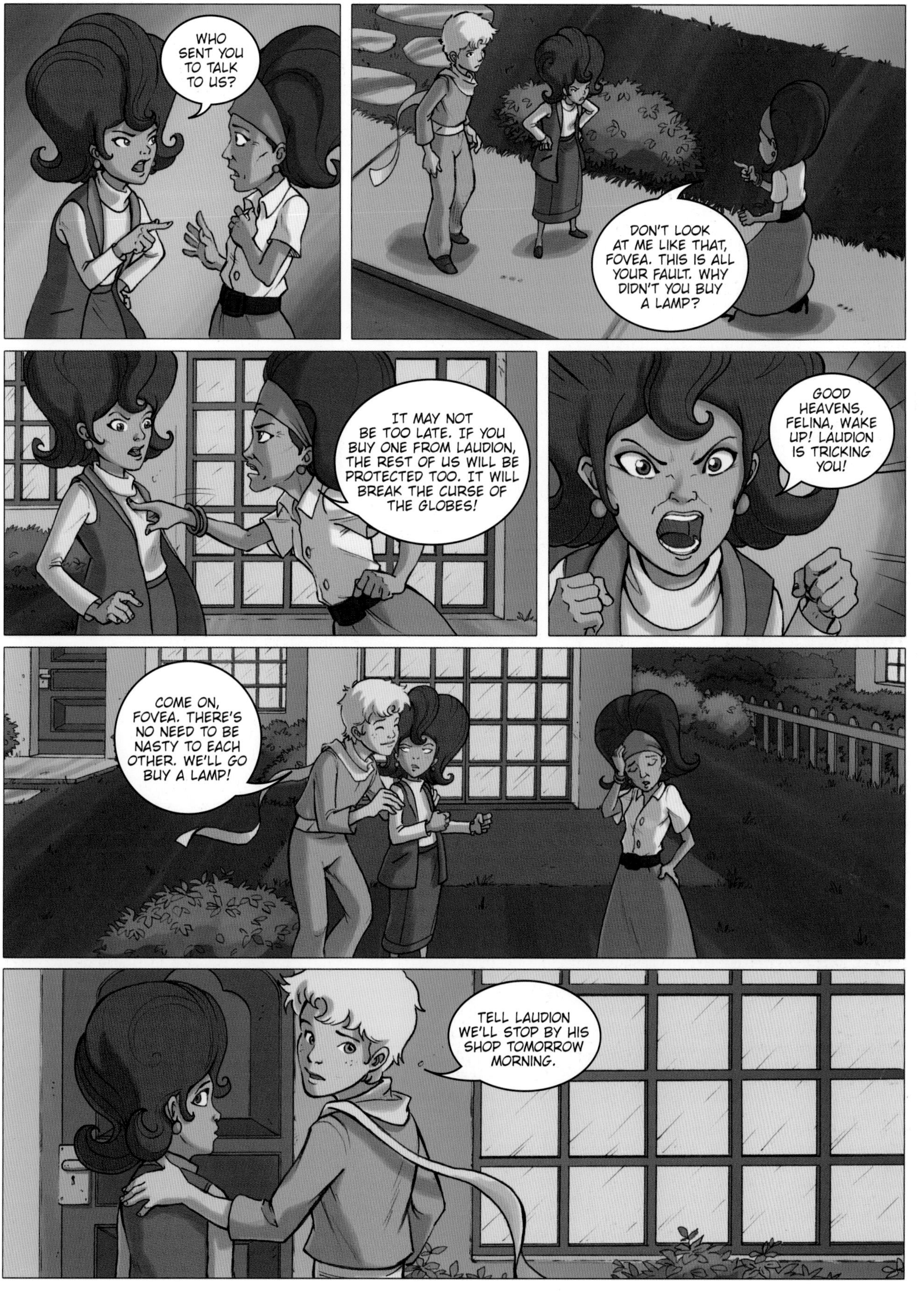
WHO SENT YOU TO TALK TO US?
DON'T LOOK AT ME LIKE THAT, FOVEA. THIS IS ALL YOUR FAULT. WHY DIDN'T YOU BUY A LAMP?
IT MAY NOT BE TOO LATE. IF YOU BUY ONE FROM LAUDION, THE REST OF US WILL BE PROTECTED TOO. IT WILL BREAK THE CURSE OF THE GLOBES!
GOOD HEAVENS, FELINA, WAKE UP! LAUDION IS TRICKING YOU!
COME ON, FOVEA. THERE'S NO NEED TO BE NASTY TO EACH OTHER. WE'LL GO BUY A LAMP!
TELL LAUDION WE'LL STOP BY HIS SHOP TOMORROW MORNING.

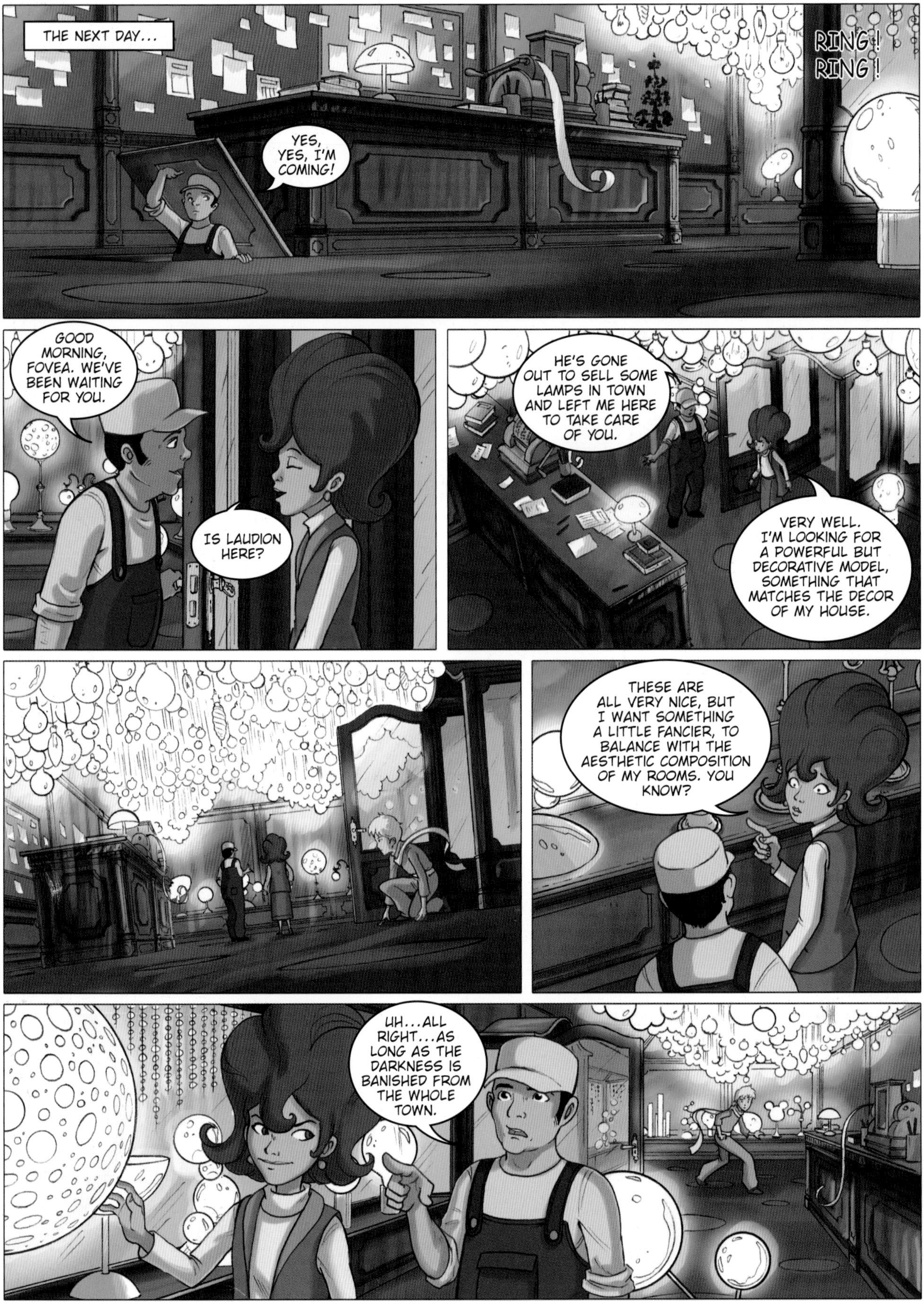
THE NEXT DAY...
RING! RING!
YES, YES, I'M COMING!
GOOD MORNING, FOVEA. WE'VE BEEN WAITING FOR YOU.
IS LAUDION HERE?
HE'S GONE OUT TO SELL SOME LAMPS IN TOWN AND LEFT ME HERE TO TAKE CARE OF YOU.
VERY WELL. I'M LOOKING FOR A POWERFUL BUT DECORATIVE MODEL, SOMETHING THAT MATCHES THE DECOR OF MY HOUSE.
THESE ARE ALL VERY NICE, BUT I WANT SOMETHING A LITTLE FANCIER, TO BALANCE WITH THE AESTHETIC COMPOSITION OF MY ROOMS. YOU KNOW?
UH...ALL RIGHT...AS LONG AS THE DARKNESS IS BANISHED FROM THE WHOLE TOWN.

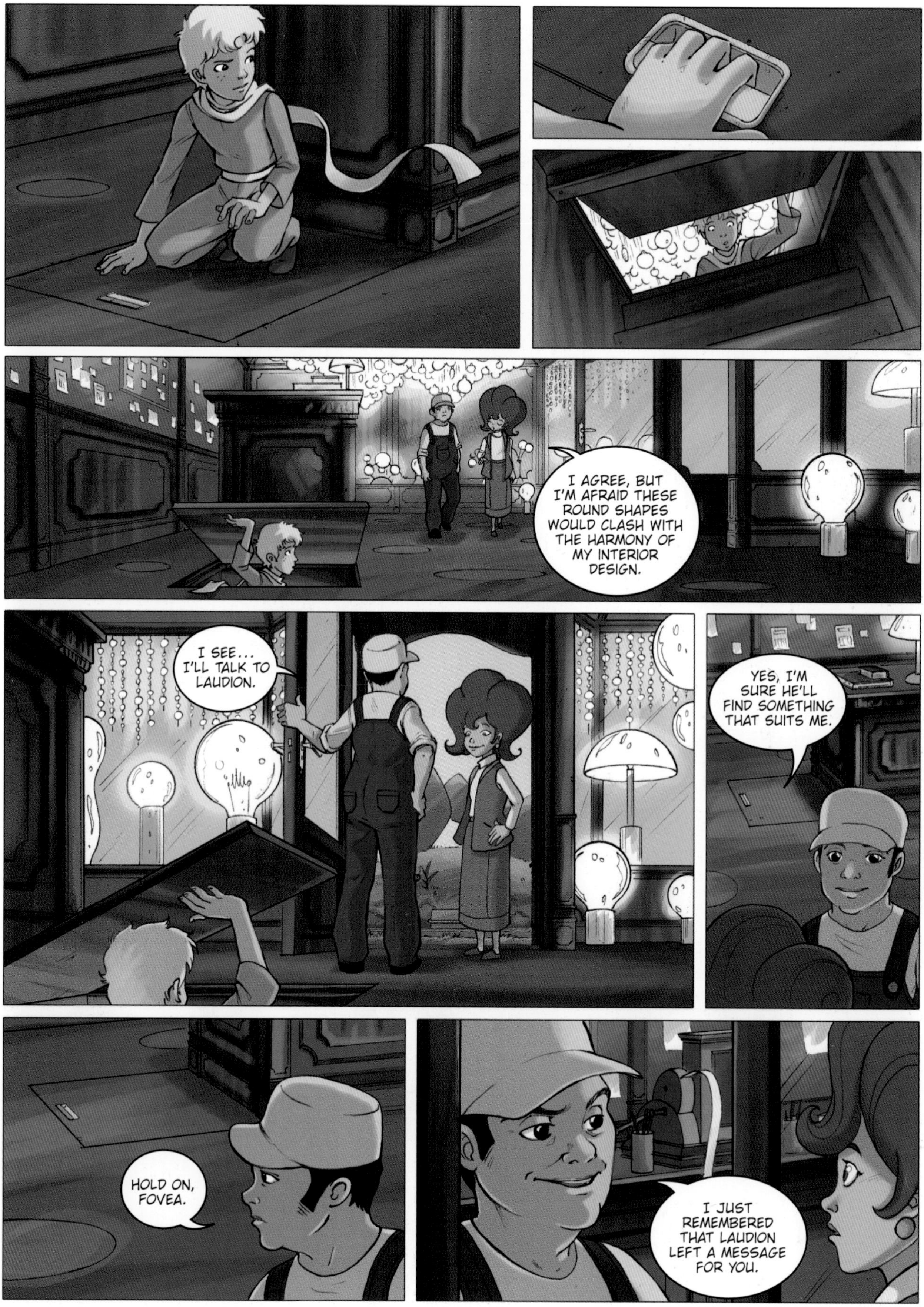
I AGREE, BUT I'M AFRAID THESE ROUND SHAPES WOULD CLASH WITH THE HARMONY OF MY INTERIOR DESIGN.
I SEE... I'LL TALK TO LAUDION.
YES, I'M SURE HE'LL FIND SOMETHING THAT SUITS ME.
HOLD ON, FOVEA.
I JUST REMEMBERED THAT LAUDION LEFT A MESSAGE FOR YOU.

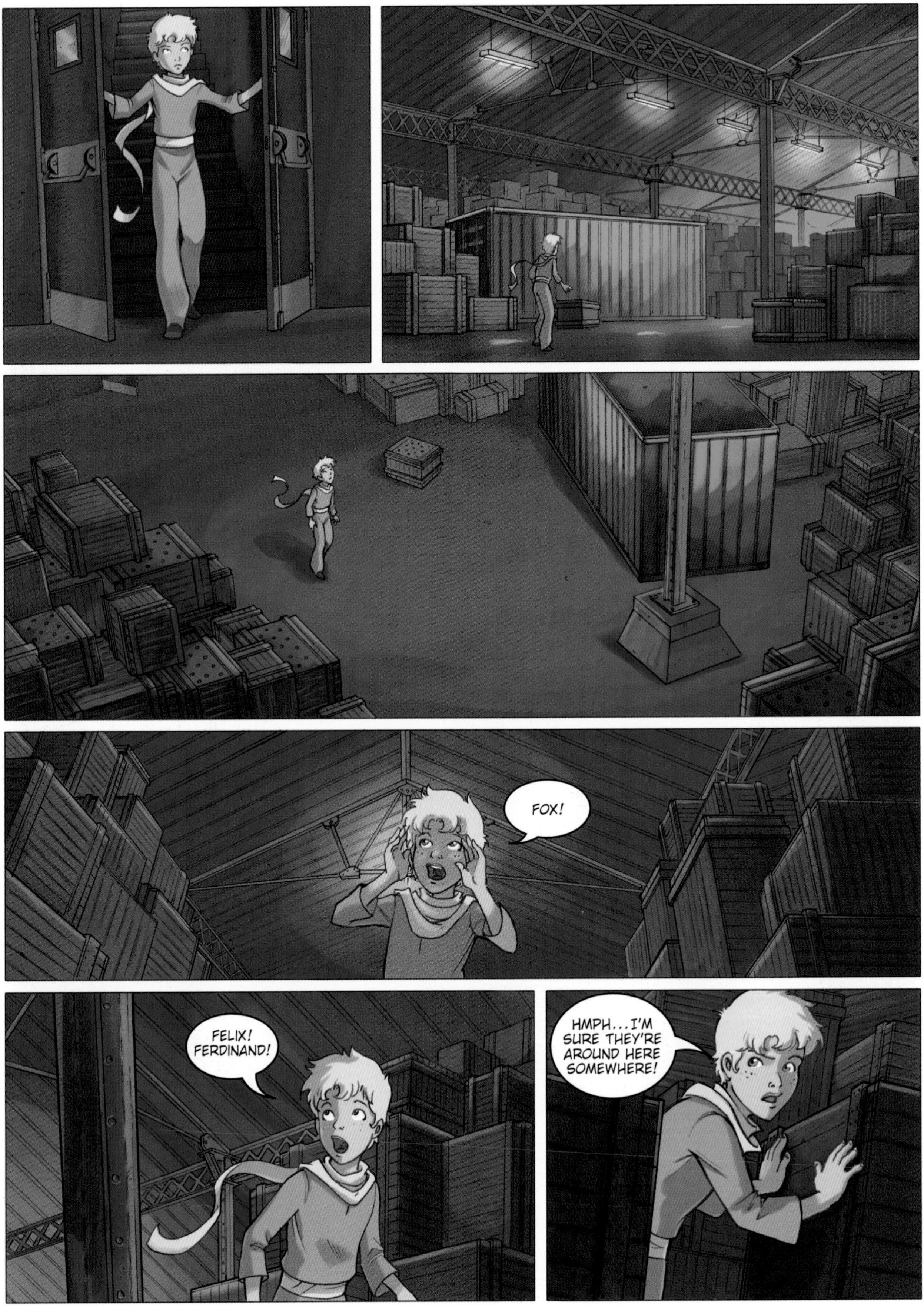
FOX!
FELIX! FERDINAND!
HMPH...I'M SURE THEY'RE AROUND HERE SOMEWHERE!

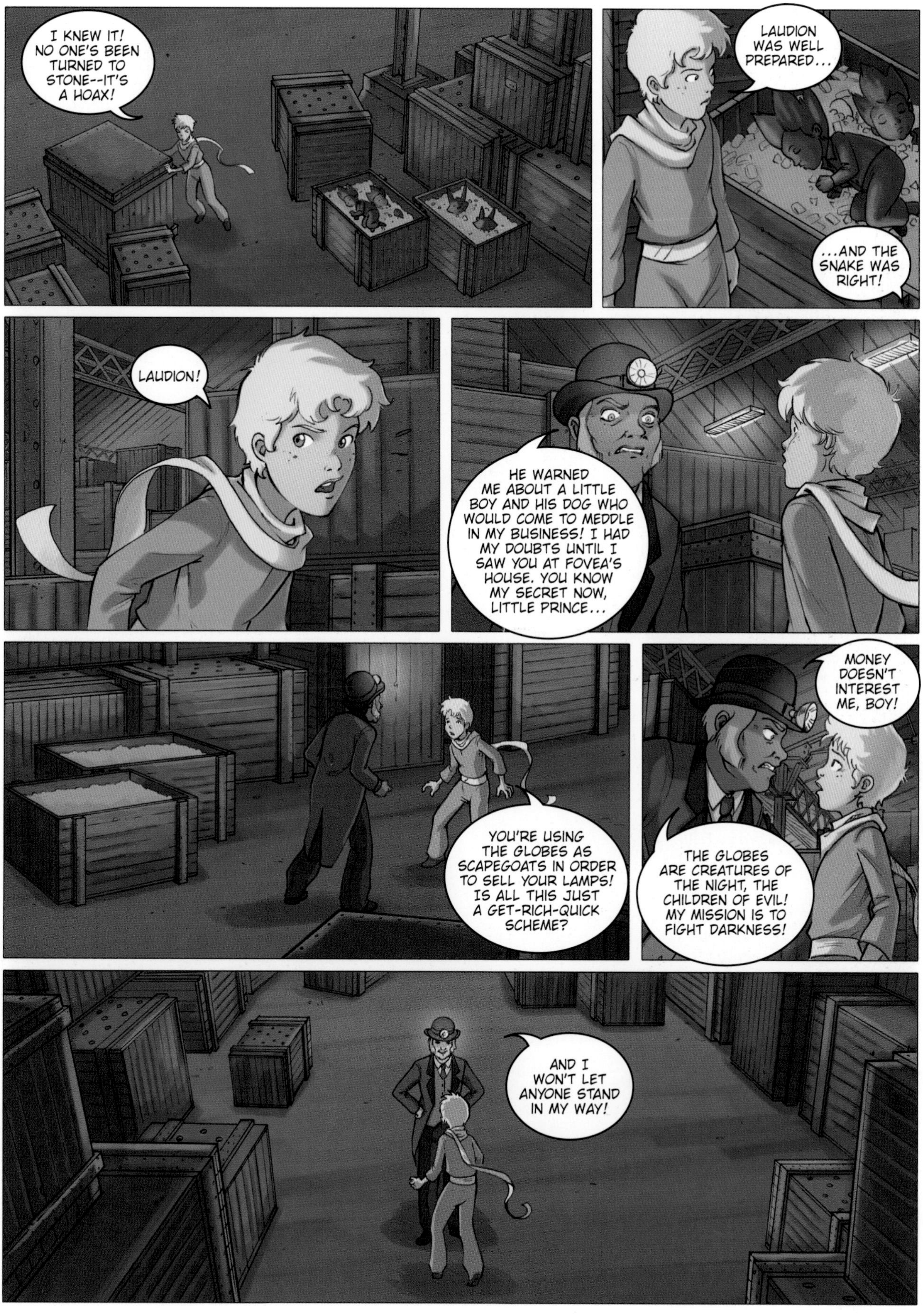
I KNEW IT! NO ONE'S BEEN TURNED TO STONE--IT'S A HOAX!
LAUDION WAS WELL PREPARED...
...AND THE SNAKE WAS RIGHT!
LAUDION!
HE WARNED ME ABOUT A LITTLE BOY AND HIS DOG WHO WOULD COME TO MEDDLE IN MY BUSINESS! I HAD MY DOUBTS UNTIL I SAW YOU AT FOVEA'S HOUSE. YOU KNOW MY SECRET NOW, LITTLE PRINCE...
YOU'RE USING THE GLOBES AS SCAPEGOATS IN ORDER TO SELL YOUR LAMPS! IS ALL THIS JUST A GET-RICH-QUICK SCHEME?
MONEY DOESN'T INTEREST ME, BOY!
THE GLOBES ARE CREATURES OF THE NIGHT, THE CHILDREN OF EVIL! MY MISSION IS TO FIGHT DARKNESS!
AND I WON'T LET ANYONE STAND IN MY WAY!

WHAT'S...

THE GLOOMIES!

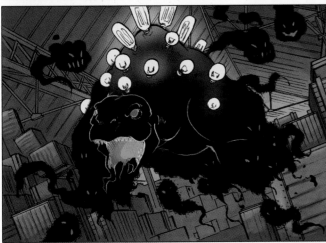

SO, LITTLE PRINCE, DO YOU STILL WANT TO PLAY HERO?

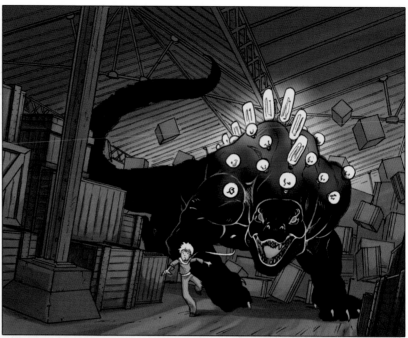

THAT SHAPE...
THEY'RE SO
MUCH STRONGER
THAN USUAL!

I USED UP
TOO MUCH
STARDUST LAST
NIGHT. I NEED
TO BUY SOME
TIME!

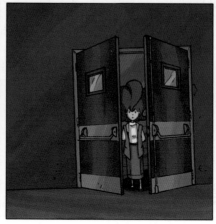

NO!

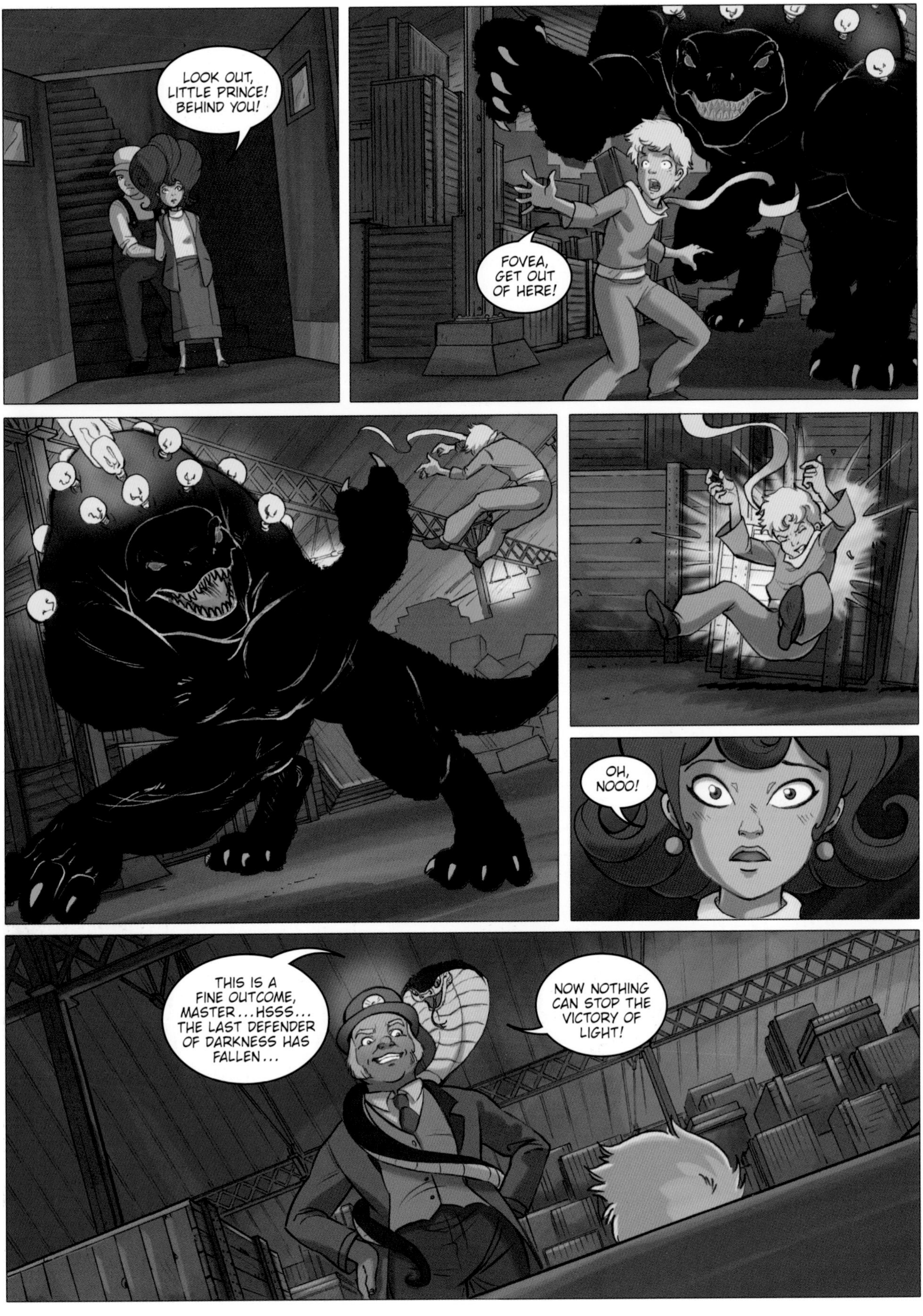

LOOK OUT, LITTLE PRINCE! BEHIND YOU!
FOVEA, GET OUT OF HERE!
OH, NOOO!
THIS IS A FINE OUTCOME, MASTER...HSSS... THE LAST DEFENDER OF DARKNESS HAS FALLEN...
NOW NOTHING CAN STOP THE VICTORY OF LIGHT!

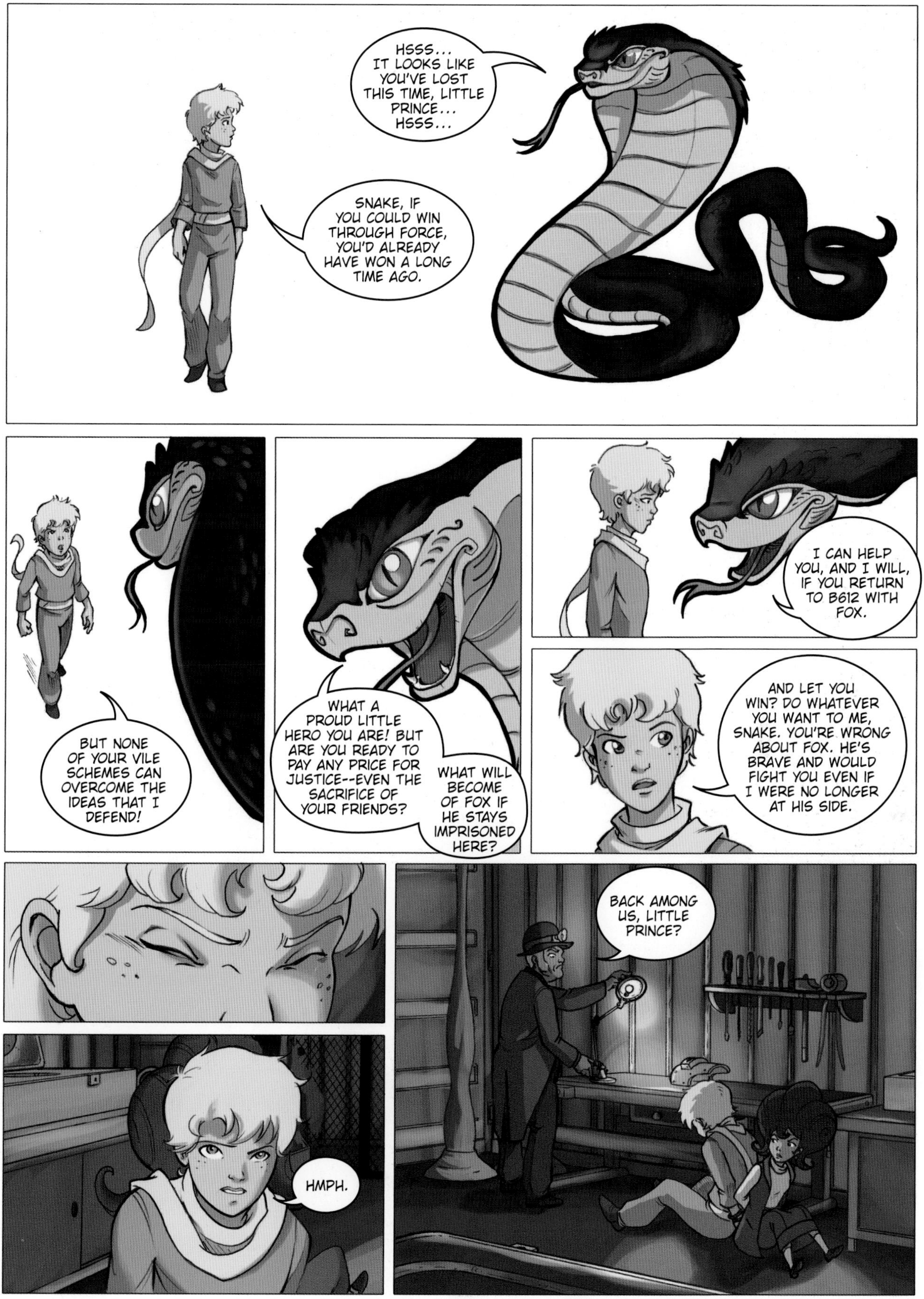
HSSS... IT LOOKS LIKE YOU'VE LOST THIS TIME, LITTLE PRINCE... HSSS...
SNAKE, IF YOU COULD WIN THROUGH FORCE, YOU'D ALREADY HAVE WON A LONG TIME AGO.
BUT NONE OF YOUR VILE SCHEMES CAN OVERCOME THE IDEAS THAT I DEFEND!
WHAT A PROUD LITTLE HERO YOU ARE! BUT ARE YOU READY TO PAY ANY PRICE FOR JUSTICE--EVEN THE SACRIFICE OF YOUR FRIENDS?
WHAT WILL BECOME OF FOX IF HE STAYS IMPRISONED HERE?
I CAN HELP YOU, AND I WILL, IF YOU RETURN TO B612 WITH FOX.
AND LET YOU WIN? DO WHATEVER YOU WANT TO ME, SNAKE. YOU'RE WRONG ABOUT FOX. HE'S BRAVE AND WOULD FIGHT YOU EVEN IF I WERE NO LONGER AT HIS SIDE.
HMPH.
BACK AMONG US, LITTLE PRINCE?

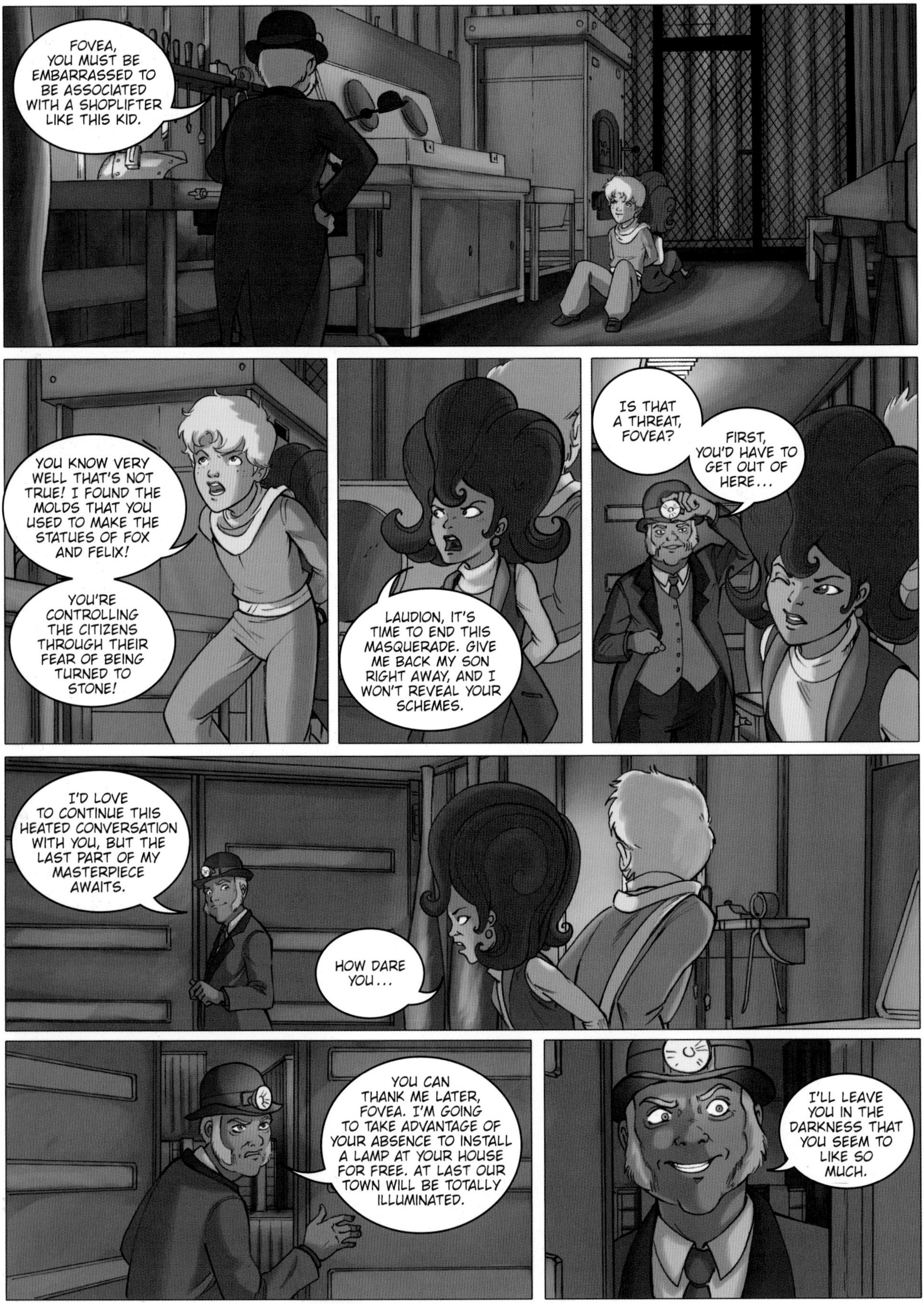
FOVEA, YOU MUST BE EMBARRASSED TO BE ASSOCIATED WITH A SHOPLIFTER LIKE THIS KID.
YOU KNOW VERY WELL THAT'S NOT TRUE! I FOUND THE MOLDS THAT YOU USED TO MAKE THE STATUES OF FOX AND FELIX!
YOU'RE CONTROLLING THE CITIZENS THROUGH THEIR FEAR OF BEING TURNED TO STONE!
LAUDION, IT'S TIME TO END THIS MASQUERADE. GIVE ME BACK MY SON RIGHT AWAY, AND I WON'T REVEAL YOUR SCHEMES.
IS THAT A THREAT, FOVEA?
FIRST, YOU'D HAVE TO GET OUT OF HERE...
I'D LOVE TO CONTINUE THIS HEATED CONVERSATION WITH YOU, BUT THE LAST PART OF MY MASTERPIECE AWAITS.
HOW DARE YOU...
YOU CAN THANK ME LATER, FOVEA. I'M GOING TO TAKE ADVANTAGE OF YOUR ABSENCE TO INSTALL A LAMP AT YOUR HOUSE FOR FREE. AT LAST OUR TOWN WILL BE TOTALLY ILLUMINATED.
I'LL LEAVE YOU IN THE DARKNESS THAT YOU SEEM TO LIKE SO MUCH.

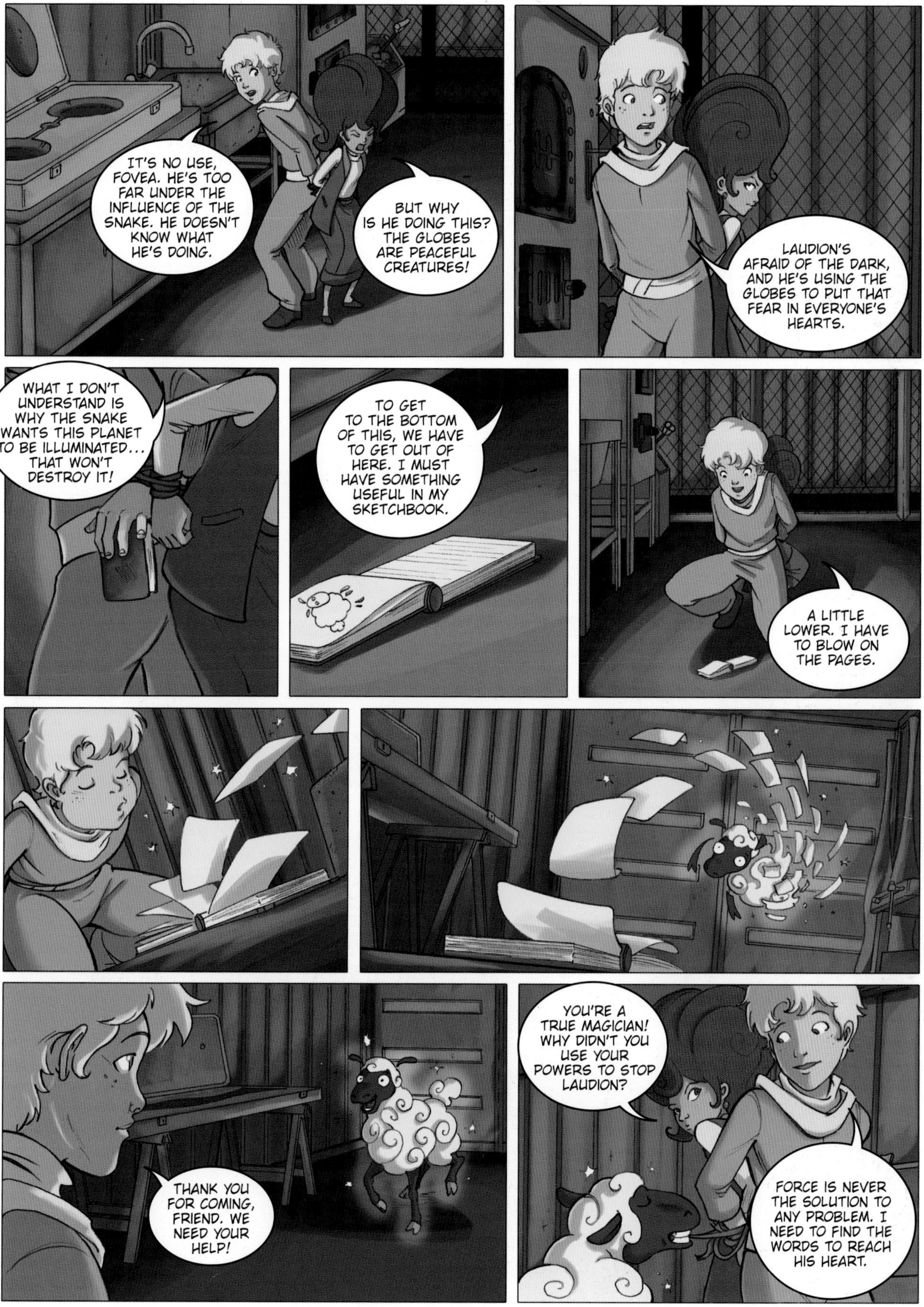
IT'S NO USE, FOVEA. HE'S TOO FAR UNDER THE INFLUENCE OF THE SNAKE. HE DOESN'T KNOW WHAT HE'S DOING.
BUT WHY IS HE DOING THIS? THE GLOBES ARE PEACEFUL CREATURES!
LAUDION'S AFRAID OF THE DARK, AND HE'S USING THE GLOBES TO PUT THAT FEAR IN EVERYONE'S HEARTS.
WHAT I DON'T UNDERSTAND IS WHY THE SNAKE WANTS THIS PLANET TO BE ILLUMINATED... THAT WON'T DESTROY IT!
TO GET TO THE BOTTOM OF THIS, WE HAVE TO GET OUT OF HERE. I MUST HAVE SOMETHING USEFUL IN MY SKETCHBOOK.
A LITTLE LOWER. I HAVE TO BLOW ON THE PAGES.
THANK YOU FOR COMING, FRIEND. WE NEED YOUR HELP!
YOU'RE A TRUE MAGICIAN! WHY DIDN'T YOU USE YOUR POWERS TO STOP LAUDION?
FORCE IS NEVER THE SOLUTION TO ANY PROBLEM. I NEED TO FIND THE WORDS TO REACH HIS HEART.

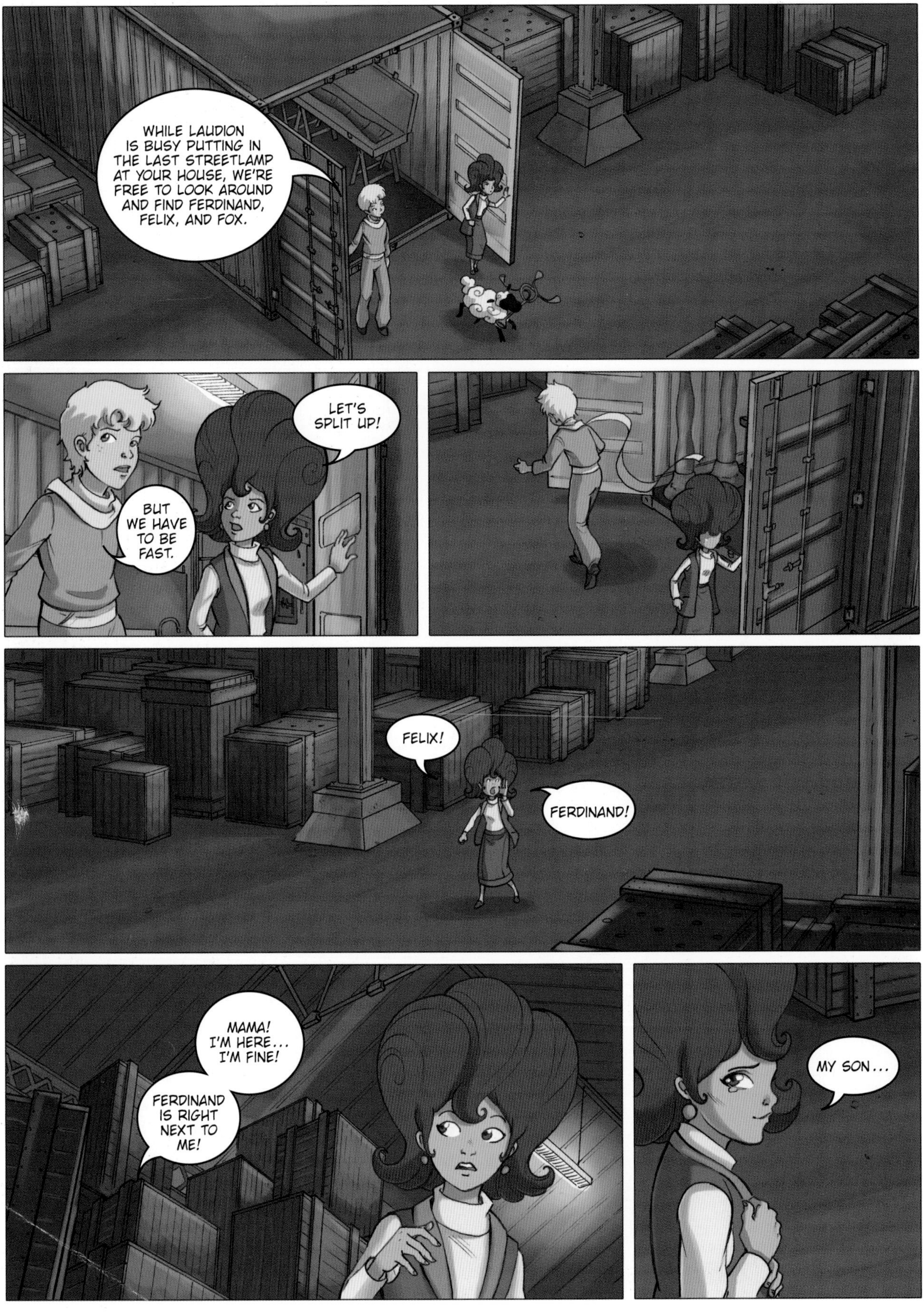
WHILE LAUDION IS BUSY PUTTING IN THE LAST STREETLAMP AT YOUR HOUSE, WE'RE FREE TO LOOK AROUND AND FIND FERDINAND, FELIX, AND FOX.
LET'S SPLIT UP!
BUT WE HAVE TO BE FAST.
FELIX!
FERDINAND!
MAMA! I'M HERE... I'M FINE!
FERDINAND IS RIGHT NEXT TO ME!
MY SON...

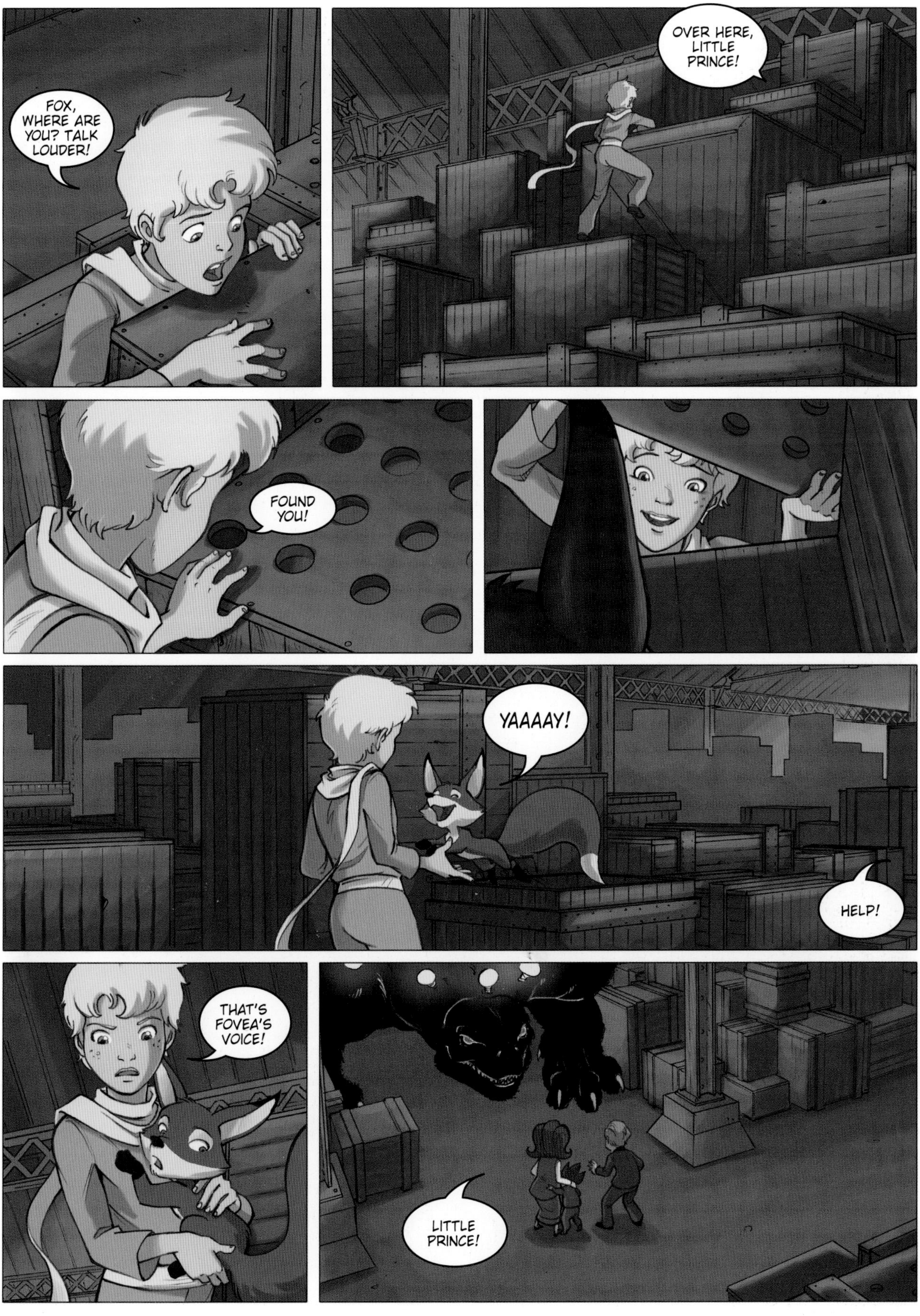
FOX, WHERE ARE YOU? TALK LOUDER!
OVER HERE, LITTLE PRINCE!
FOUND YOU!
YAAAAY!
HELP!
THAT'S FOVEA'S VOICE!
LITTLE PRINCE!

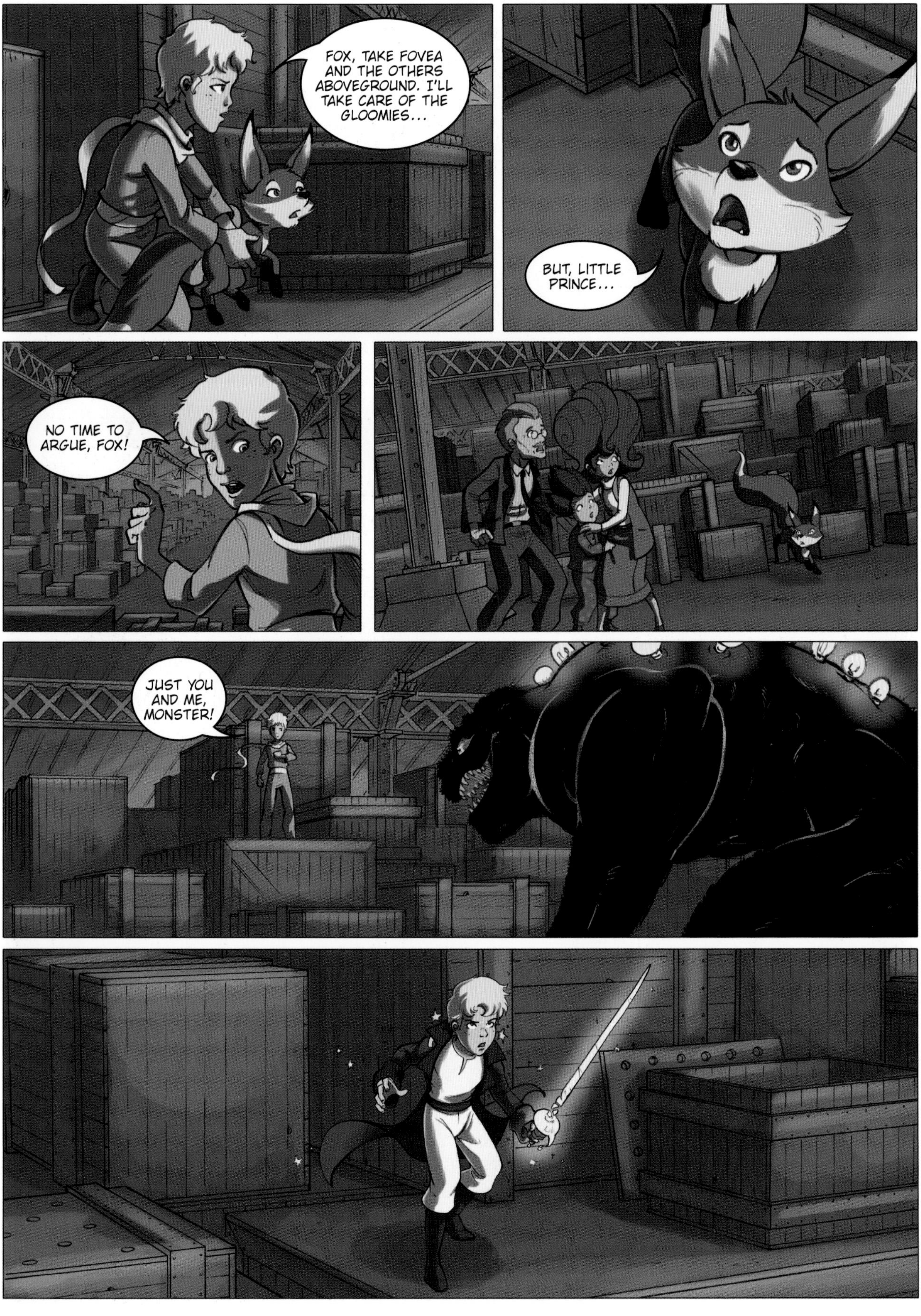
FOX, TAKE FOVEA AND THE OTHERS ABOVEGROUND. I'LL TAKE CARE OF THE GLOOMIES...
BUT, LITTLE PRINCE...
NO TIME TO ARGUE, FOX!
JUST YOU AND ME, MONSTER!

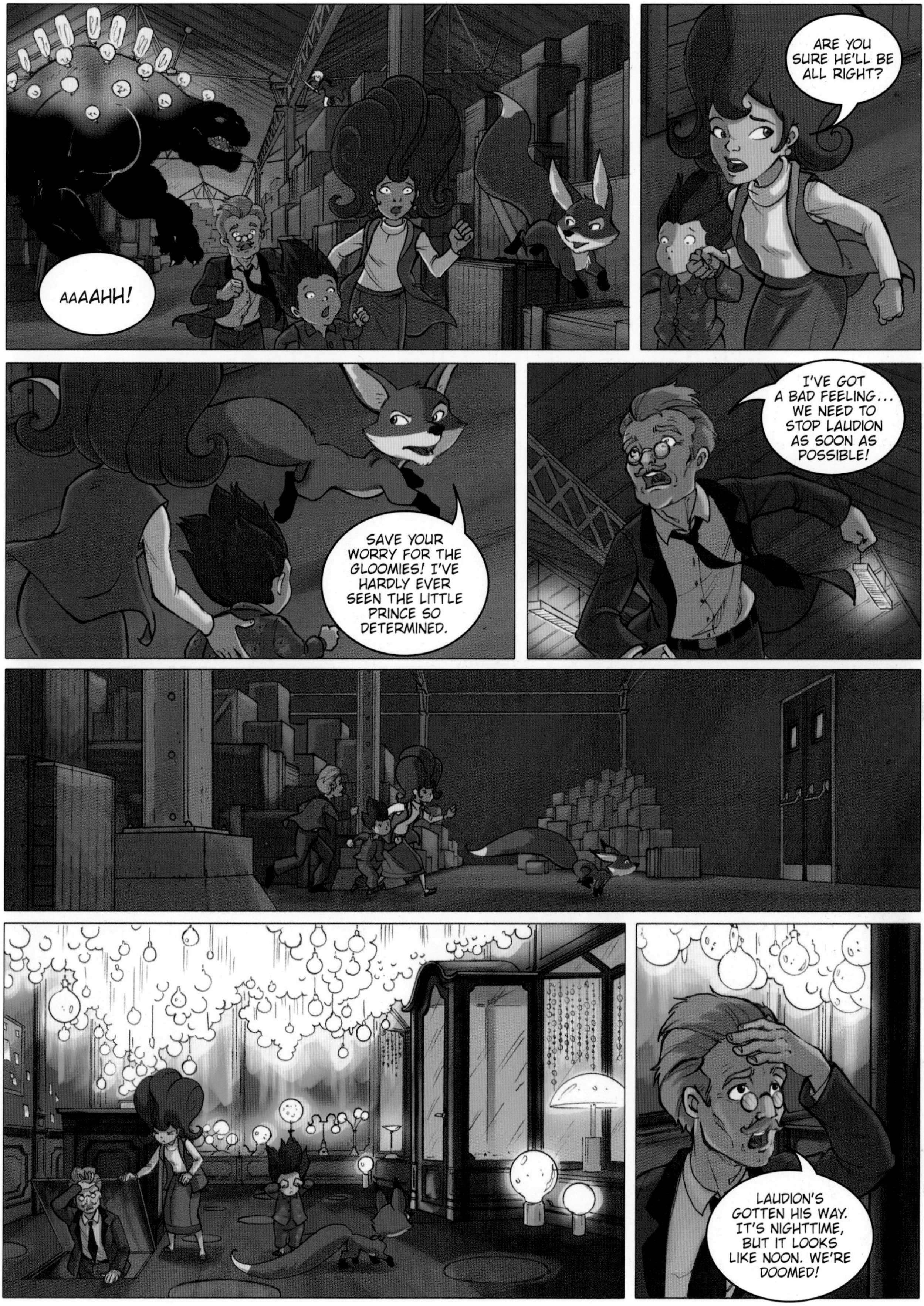
AAAAHH!
ARE YOU SURE HE'LL BE ALL RIGHT?
SAVE YOUR WORRY FOR THE GLOOMIES! I'VE HARDLY EVER SEEN THE LITTLE PRINCE SO DETERMINED.
I'VE GOT A BAD FEELING... WE NEED TO STOP LAUDION AS SOON AS POSSIBLE!
LAUDION'S GOTTEN HIS WAY. IT'S NIGHTTIME, BUT IT LOOKS LIKE NOON. WE'RE DOOMED!

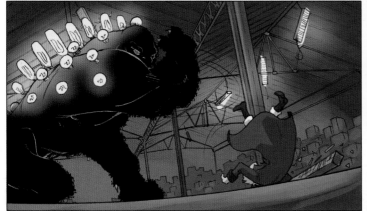

LET'S GO!

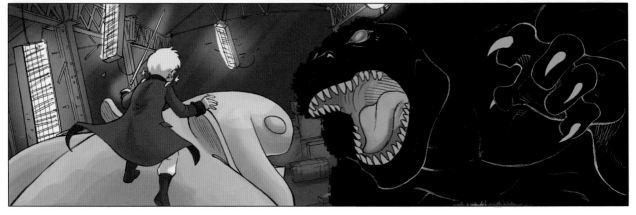

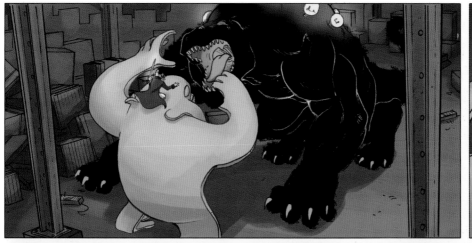

HOLD ON TIGHT. I HAVE AN IDEA!

YAAH!!!

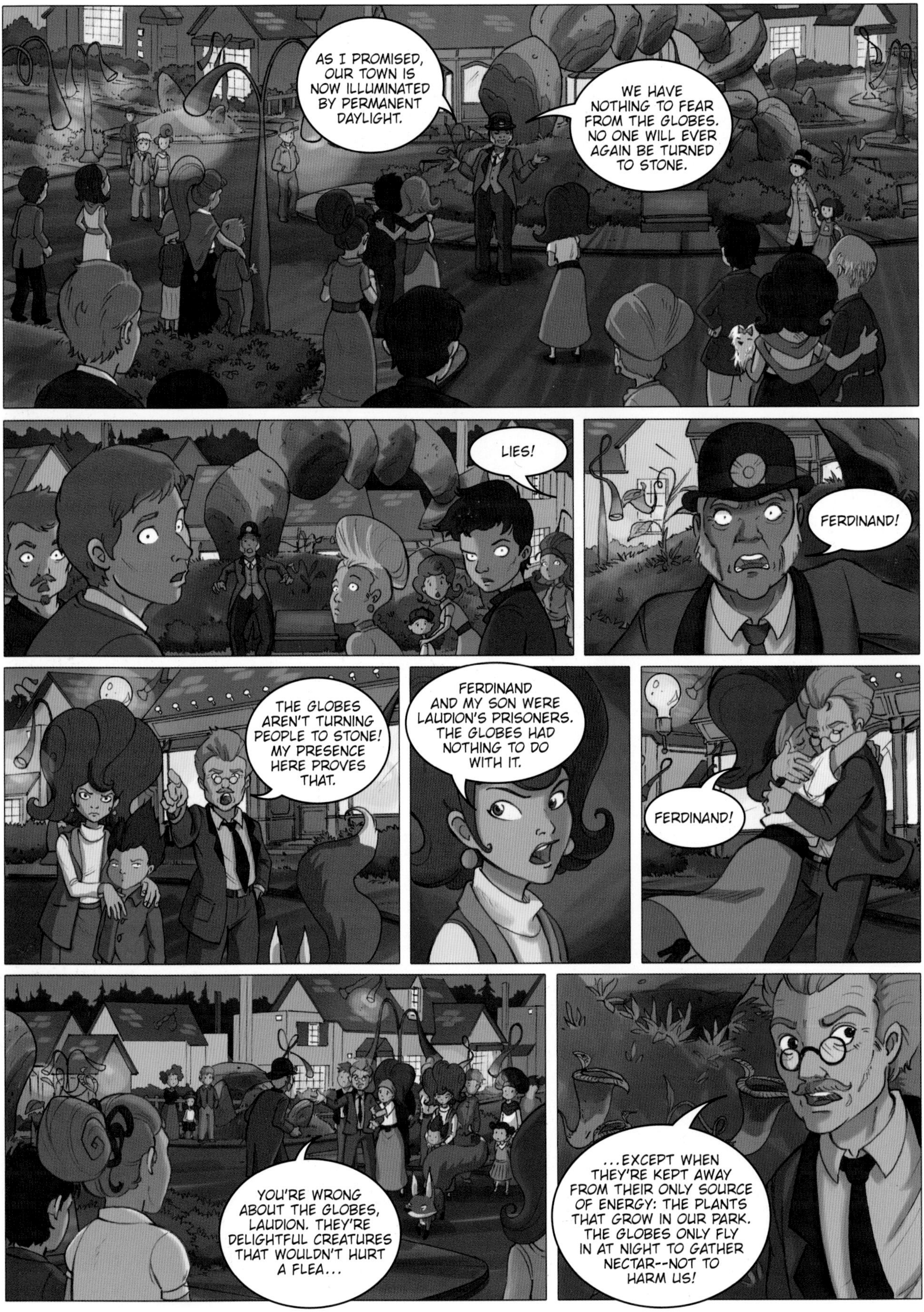
AS I PROMISED, OUR TOWN IS NOW ILLUMINATED BY PERMANENT DAYLIGHT.
WE HAVE NOTHING TO FEAR FROM THE GLOBES. NO ONE WILL EVER AGAIN BE TURNED TO STONE.
LIES!
FERDINAND!
THE GLOBES AREN'T TURNING PEOPLE TO STONE! MY PRESENCE HERE PROVES THAT.
FERDINAND AND MY SON WERE LAUDION'S PRISONERS. THE GLOBES HAD NOTHING TO DO WITH IT.
FERDINAND!
YOU'RE WRONG ABOUT THE GLOBES, LAUDION. THEY'RE DELIGHTFUL CREATURES THAT WOULDN'T HURT A FLEA...
...EXCEPT WHEN THEY'RE KEPT AWAY FROM THEIR ONLY SOURCE OF ENERGY: THE PLANTS THAT GROW IN OUR PARK. THE GLOBES ONLY FLY IN AT NIGHT TO GATHER NECTAR--NOT TO HARM US!

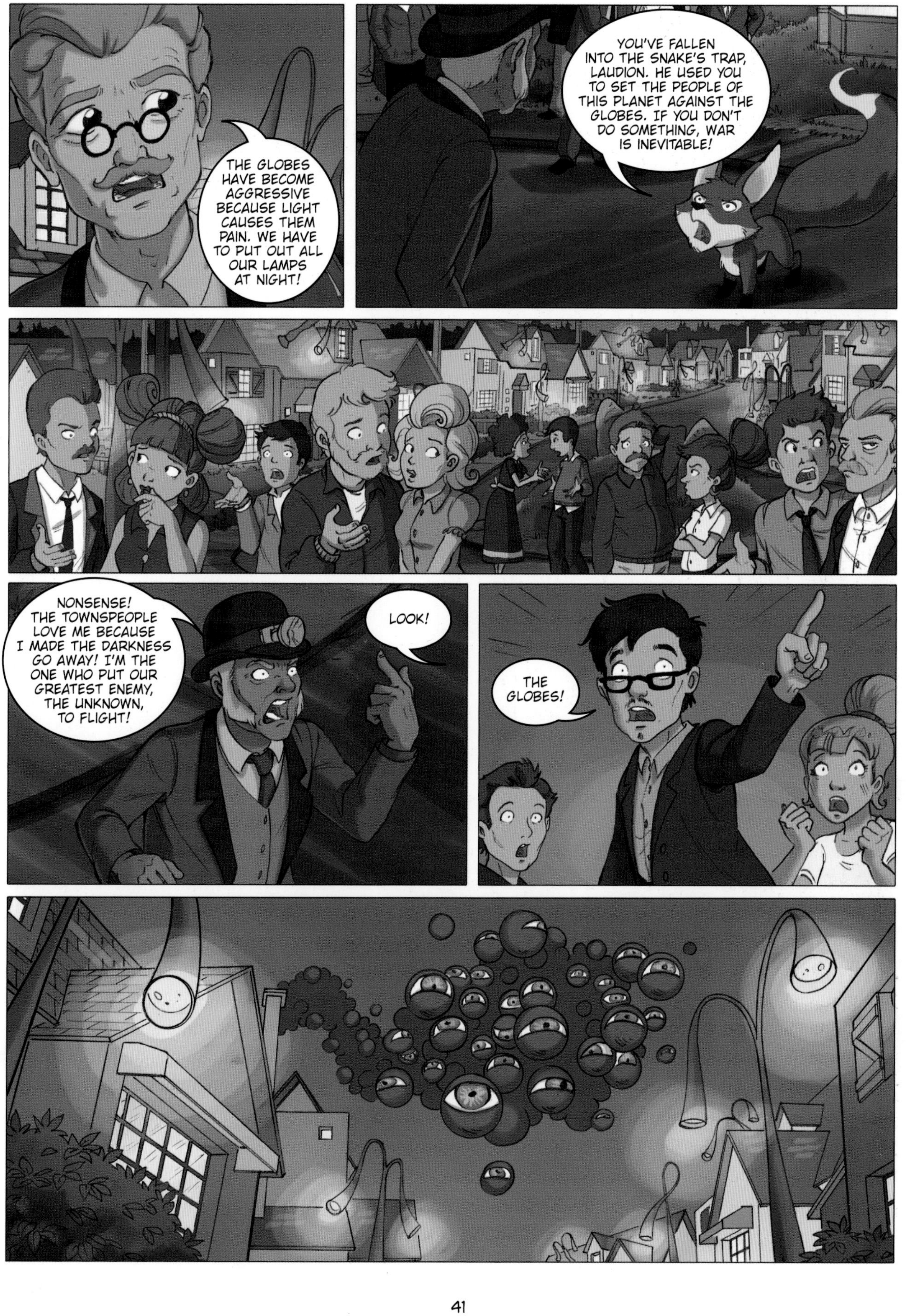
THE GLOBES HAVE BECOME AGGRESSIVE BECAUSE LIGHT CAUSES THEM PAIN. WE HAVE TO PUT OUT ALL OUR LAMPS AT NIGHT!
YOU'VE FALLEN INTO THE SNAKE'S TRAP, LAUDION. HE USED YOU TO SET THE PEOPLE OF THIS PLANET AGAINST THE GLOBES. IF YOU DON'T DO SOMETHING, WAR IS INEVITABLE!
NONSENSE! THE TOWNSPEOPLE LOVE ME BECAUSE I MADE THE DARKNESS GO AWAY! I'M THE ONE WHO PUT OUR GREATEST ENEMY, THE UNKNOWN, TO FLIGHT!
LOOK!
THE GLOBES!

STAY CALM! THEY'RE NOT DANGEROUS.

WE'LL NEVER PUT OUT ALL THESE AWFUL STREETLAMPS IN TIME!

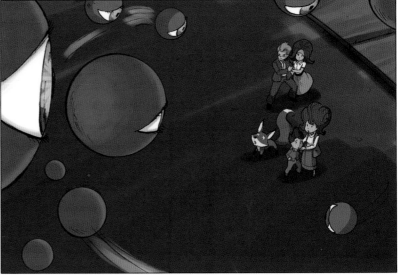

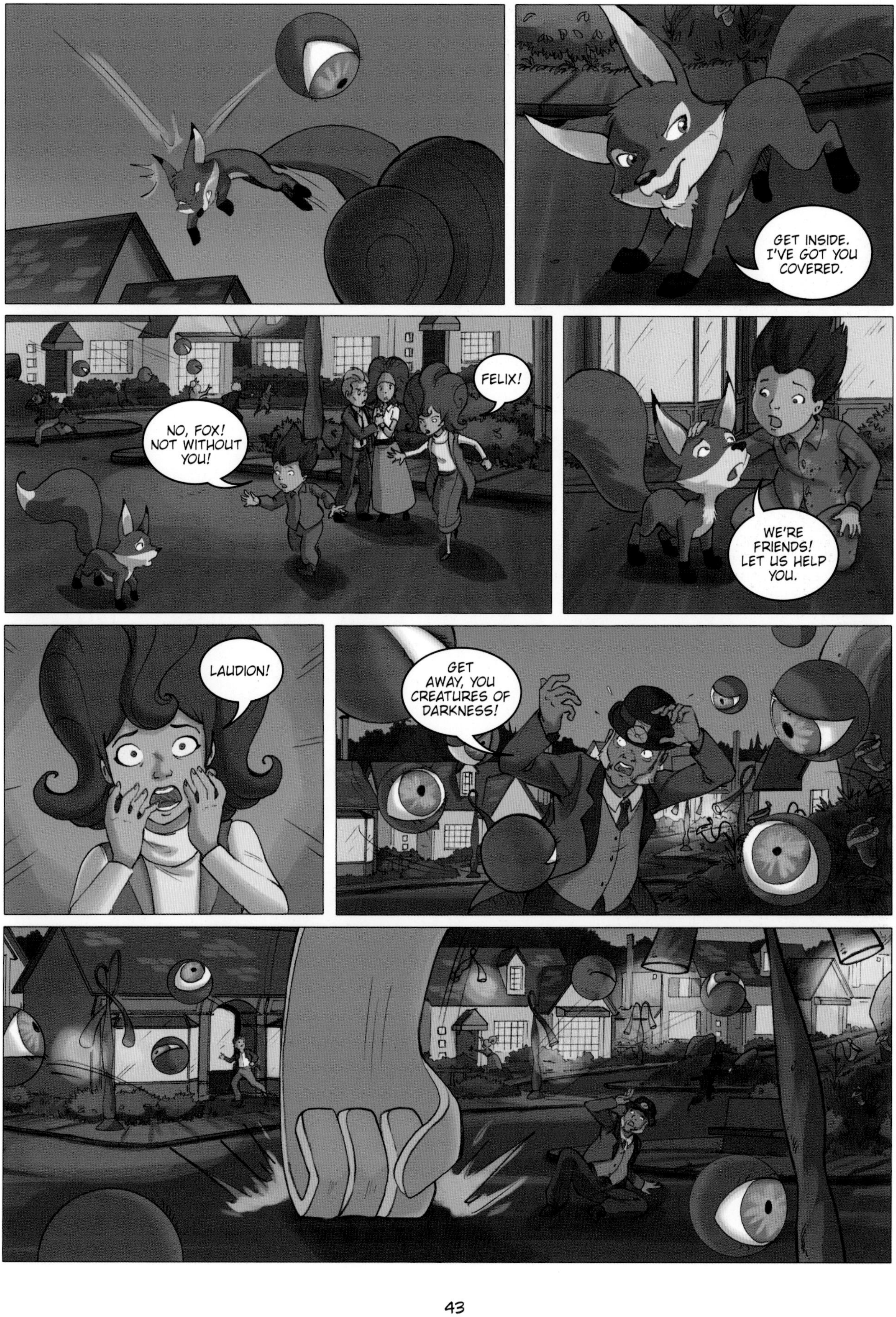
GET INSIDE. I'VE GOT YOU COVERED.
FELIX!
NO, FOX! NOT WITHOUT YOU!
WE'RE FRIENDS! LET US HELP YOU.
LAUDION!
GET AWAY, YOU CREATURES OF DARKNESS!

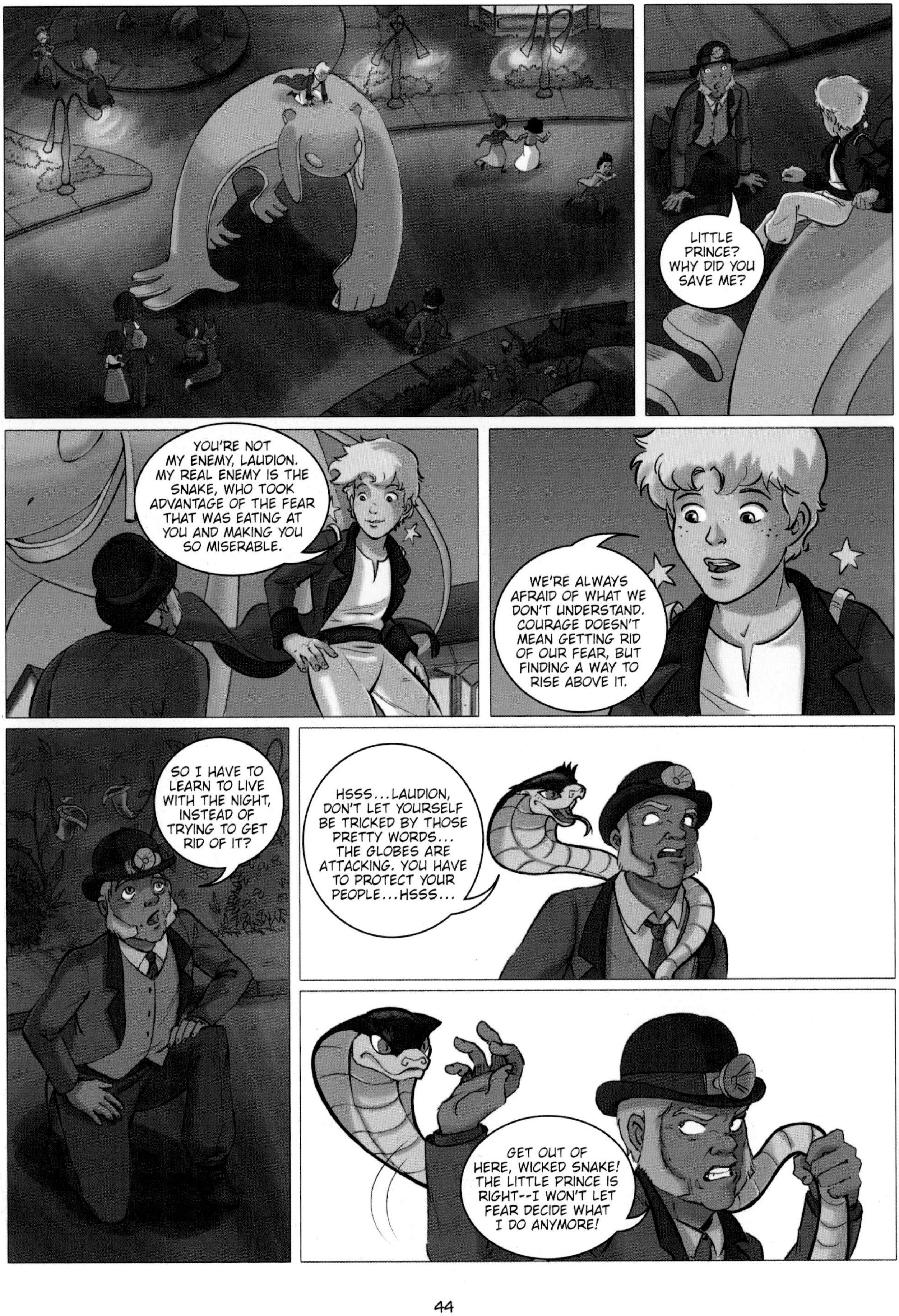

LITTLE PRINCE? WHY DID YOU SAVE ME?
YOU'RE NOT MY ENEMY, LAUDION. MY REAL ENEMY IS THE SNAKE, WHO TOOK ADVANTAGE OF THE FEAR THAT WAS EATING AT YOU AND MAKING YOU SO MISERABLE.
WE'RE ALWAYS AFRAID OF WHAT WE DON'T UNDERSTAND. COURAGE DOESN'T MEAN GETTING RID OF OUR FEAR, BUT FINDING A WAY TO RISE ABOVE IT.
SO I HAVE TO LEARN TO LIVE WITH THE NIGHT, INSTEAD OF TRYING TO GET RID OF IT?
HSSS...LAUDION, DON'T LET YOURSELF BE TRICKED BY THOSE PRETTY WORDS... THE GLOBES ARE ATTACKING. YOU HAVE TO PROTECT YOUR PEOPLE...HSSS...
GET OUT OF HERE, WICKED SNAKE! THE LITTLE PRINCE IS RIGHT--I WON'T LET FEAR DECIDE WHAT I DO ANYMORE!

IT'S ALL MY FAULT, LITTLE PRINCE...TELL ME HOW I CAN MAKE UP FOR IT.

IS THERE ANY WAY TO SHUT OFF ALL THE LIGHTS AT ONCE?

THEN THE GLOBES WOULD CALM DOWN AND STOP ATTACKING...

OF COURSE! ALL THE STREETLAMPS ARE CONNECTED TO A GENERATOR IN MY WAREHOUSE. IT'S A SAFETY MEASURE.

PERFECT. I'LL KEEP THE GLOBES BUSY WHILE YOU SHUT DOWN THE GENERATOR.

YOU'RE SURE? ALL ALONE?

DON'T WORRY. WE'VE GOT IT COVERED.

THANK YOU FOR TRUSTING IN ME.

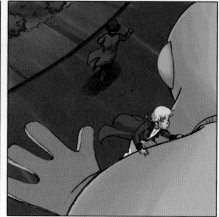

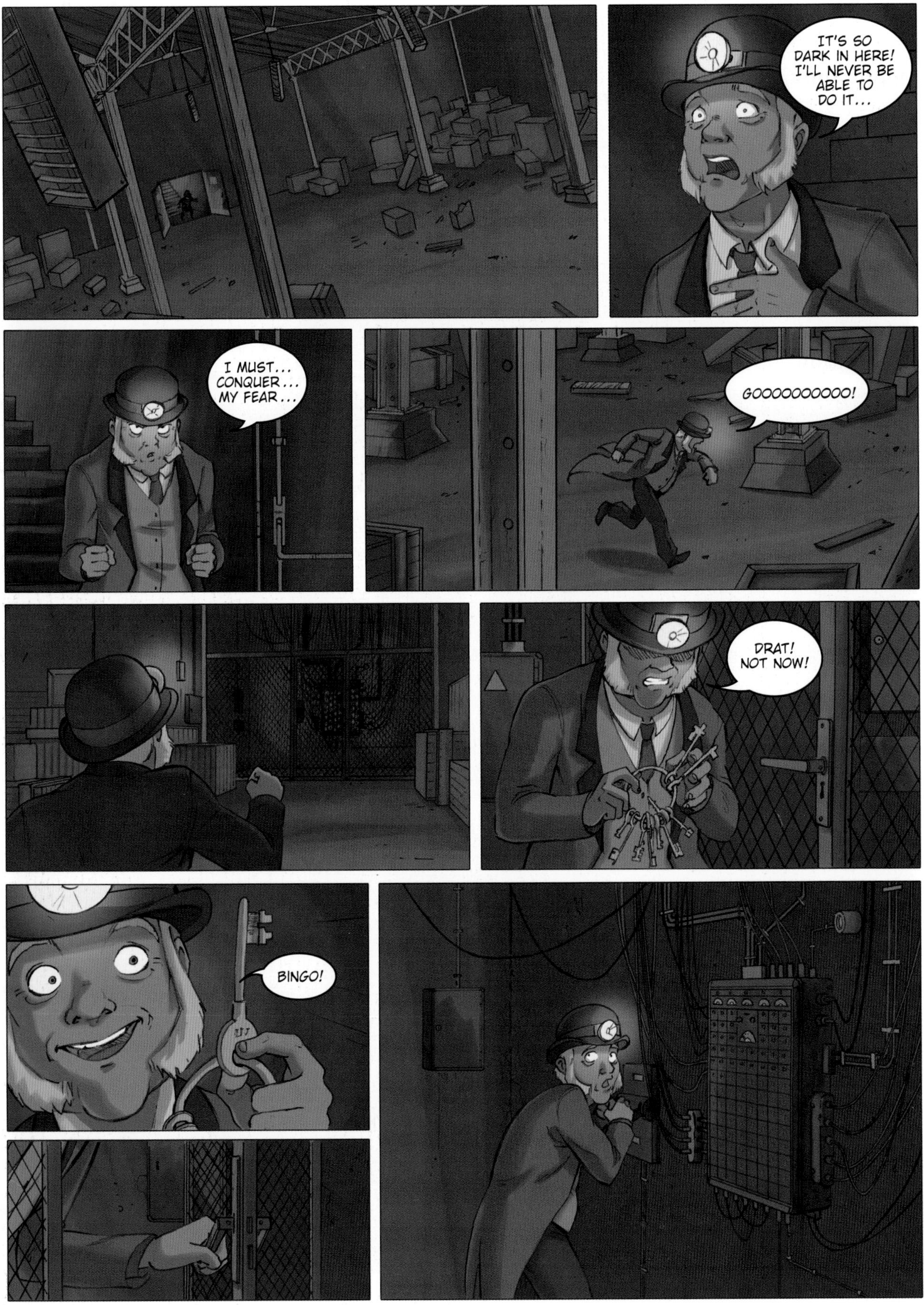
IT'S SO DARK IN HERE! I'LL NEVER BE ABLE TO DO IT...
I MUST... CONQUER... MY FEAR...
GOOOOOOOOOO!
DRAT! NOT NOW!
BINGO!

I'M ALL OUT OF STARDUST. NO MORE TRANSFORMATIONS.

SO... THIS IS THE END...

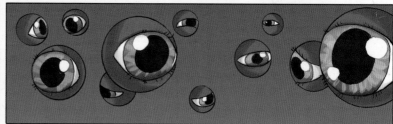

LAUDION DID IT!

WELL, LAUDION, IT LOOKS LIKE YOU'VE SAVED YOUR PLANET!

YES...THANK YOU, LITTLE PRINCE. I'VE LEARNED TO ACCEPT MY FEAR.

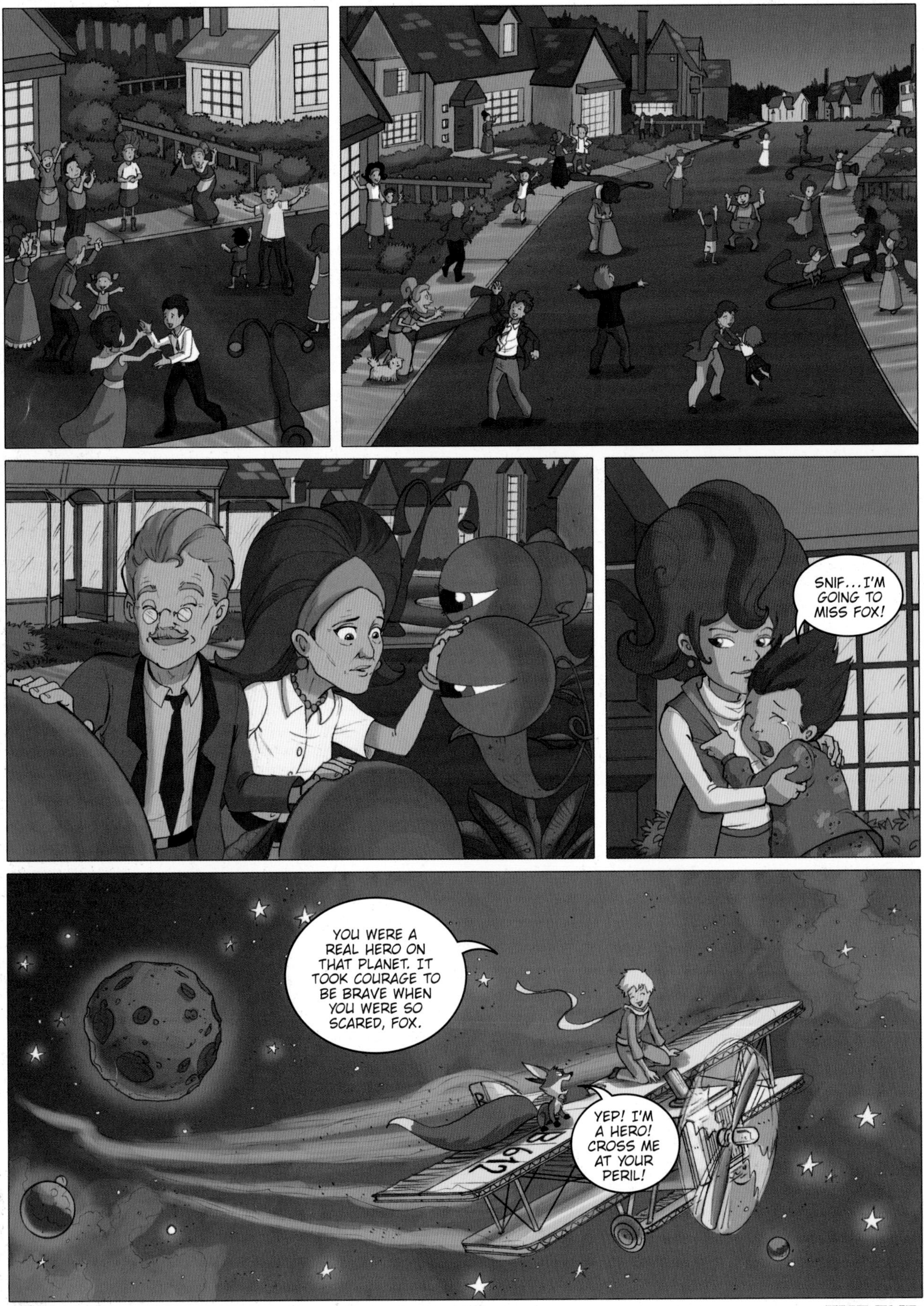
SNIF... I'M GOING TO MISS FOX!
YOU WERE A REAL HERO ON THAT PLANET. IT TOOK COURAGE TO BE BRAVE WHEN YOU WERE SO SCARED, FOX.
YEP! I'M A HERO! CROSS ME AT YOUR PERIL!
B 612

THE END

The Little Prince

AS IMAGINED BY
OLIVIER SUPIOT

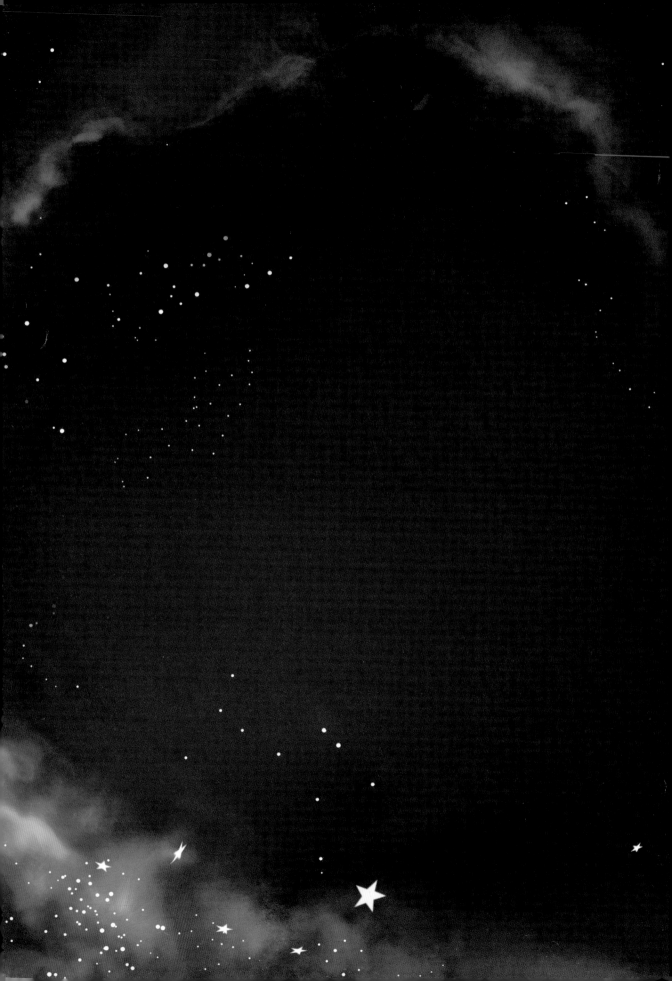

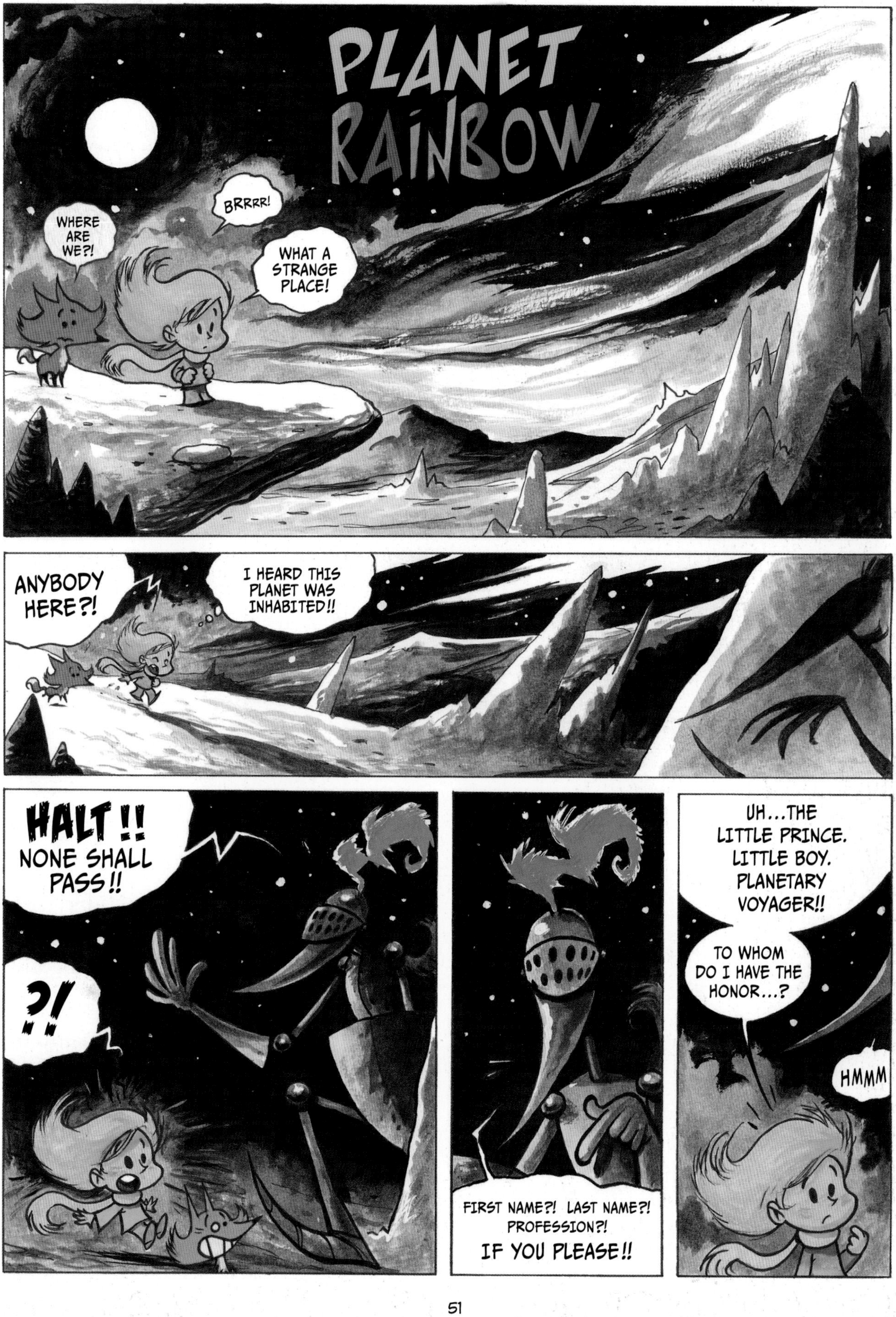
PLANET RAINBOW
WHERE ARE WE?!
BRRRR!
WHAT A STRANGE PLACE!
ANYBODY HERE?!
I HEARD THIS PLANET WAS INHABITED!!
HALT!! NONE SHALL PASS!!
?!
FIRST NAME?! LAST NAME?! PROFESSION?!
IF YOU PLEASE!!
UH...THE LITTLE PRINCE. LITTLE BOY. PLANETARY VOYAGER!!
TO WHOM DO I HAVE THE HONOR...?
HMMM

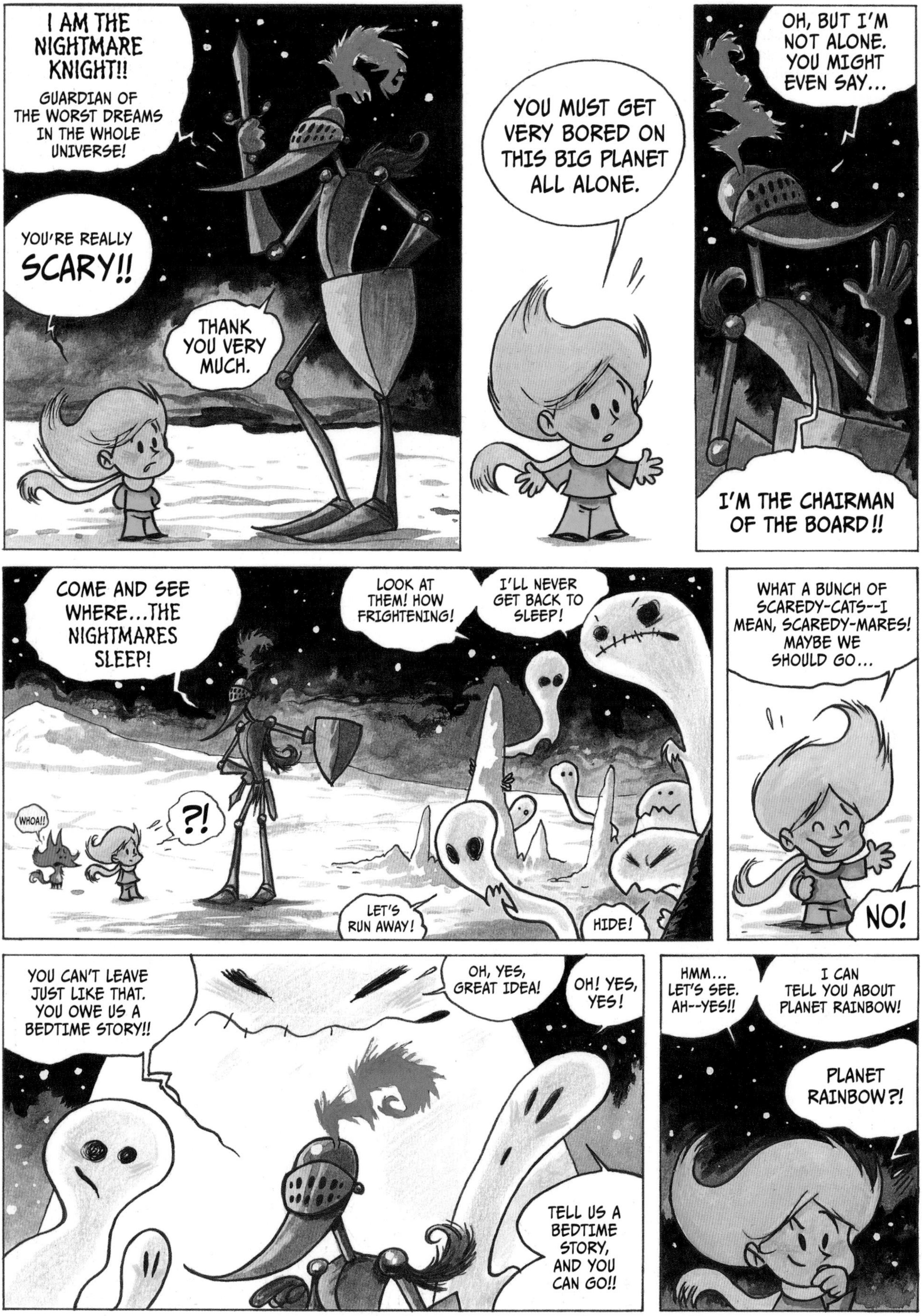
I AM THE NIGHTMARE KNIGHT!!
GUARDIAN OF THE WORST DREAMS IN THE WHOLE UNIVERSE!
YOU'RE REALLY SCARY!!
THANK YOU VERY MUCH.
YOU MUST GET VERY BORED ON THIS BIG PLANET ALL ALONE.
OH, BUT I'M NOT ALONE. YOU MIGHT EVEN SAY...
I'M THE CHAIRMAN OF THE BOARD!!
COME AND SEE WHERE...THE NIGHTMARES SLEEP!
LOOK AT THEM! HOW FRIGHTENING!
I'LL NEVER GET BACK TO SLEEP!
WHOA!!
?!
LET'S RUN AWAY!
HIDE!
WHAT A BUNCH OF SCAREDY-CATS--I MEAN, SCAREDY-MARES! MAYBE WE SHOULD GO...
NO!
YOU CAN'T LEAVE JUST LIKE THAT. YOU OWE US A BEDTIME STORY!!
OH, YES, GREAT IDEA!
OH! YES, YES!
TELL US A BEDTIME STORY, AND YOU CAN GO!!
HMM... LET'S SEE. AH--YES!!
I CAN TELL YOU ABOUT PLANET RAINBOW!
PLANET RAINBOW?!

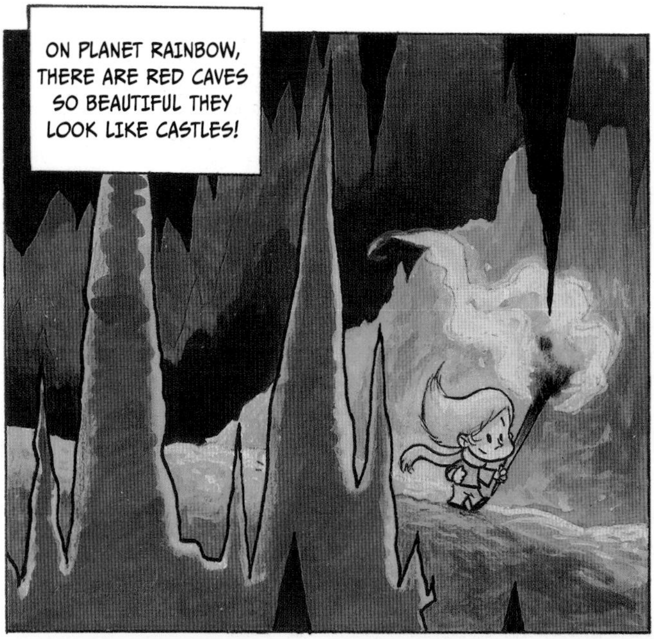
ON PLANET RAINBOW, THERE ARE RED CAVES SO BEAUTIFUL THEY LOOK LIKE CASTLES!

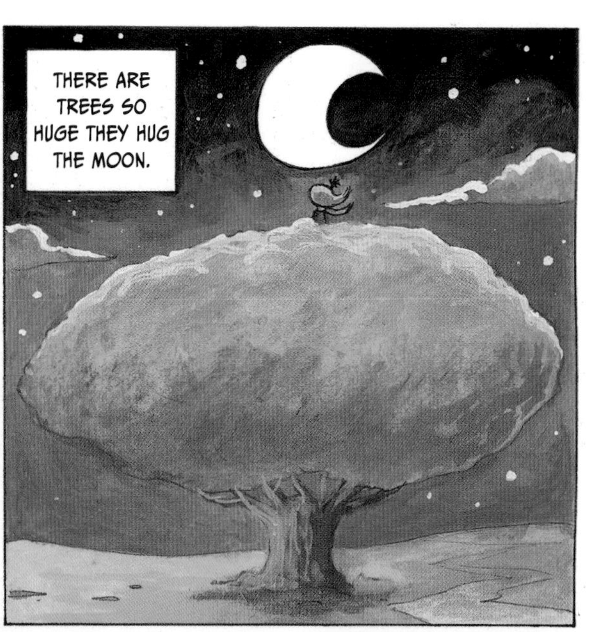
THERE ARE TREES SO HUGE THEY HUG THE MOON.

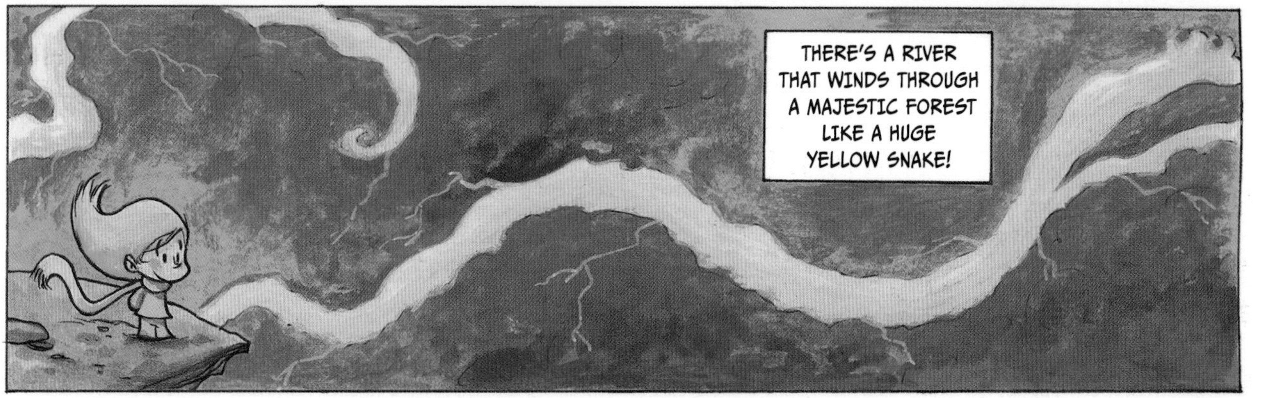
THERE'S A RIVER THAT WINDS THROUGH A MAJESTIC FOREST LIKE A HUGE YELLOW SNAKE!

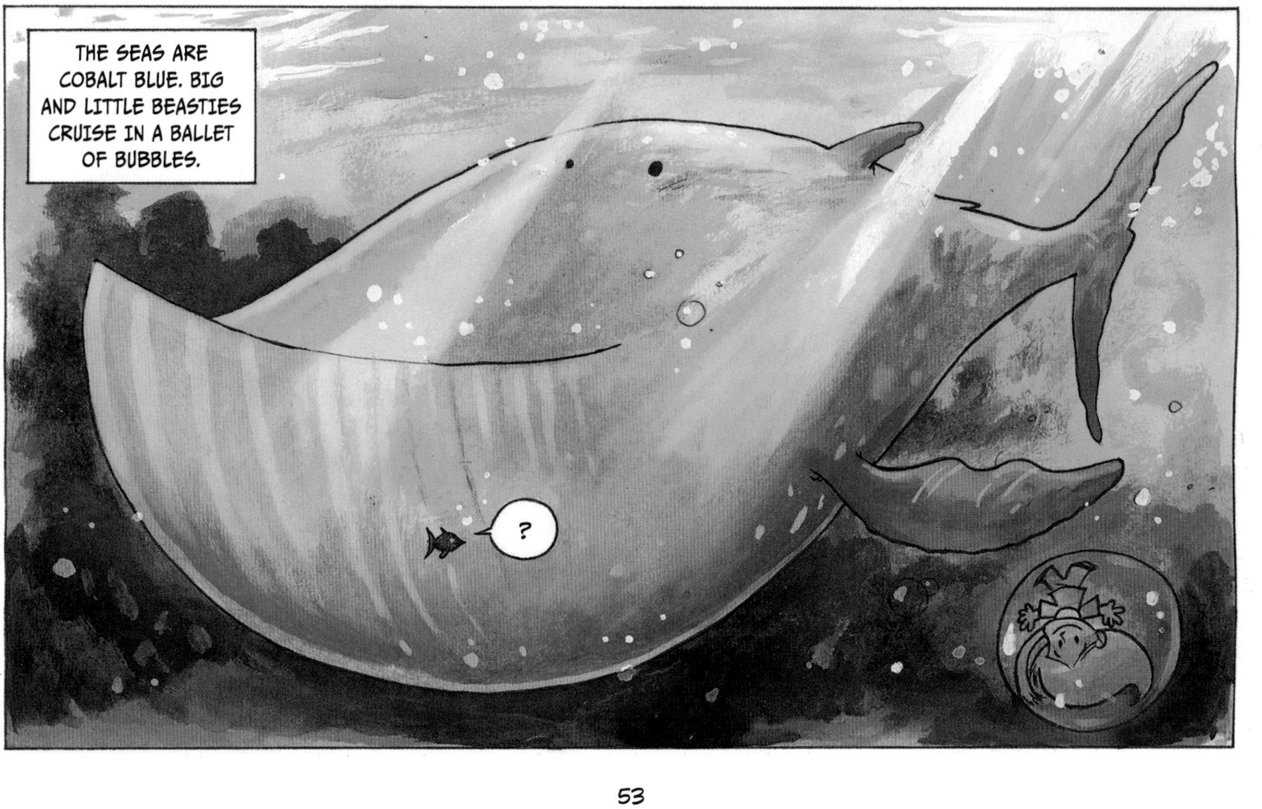
THE SEAS ARE COBALT BLUE. BIG AND LITTLE BEASTIES CRUISE IN A BALLET OF BUBBLES.
?

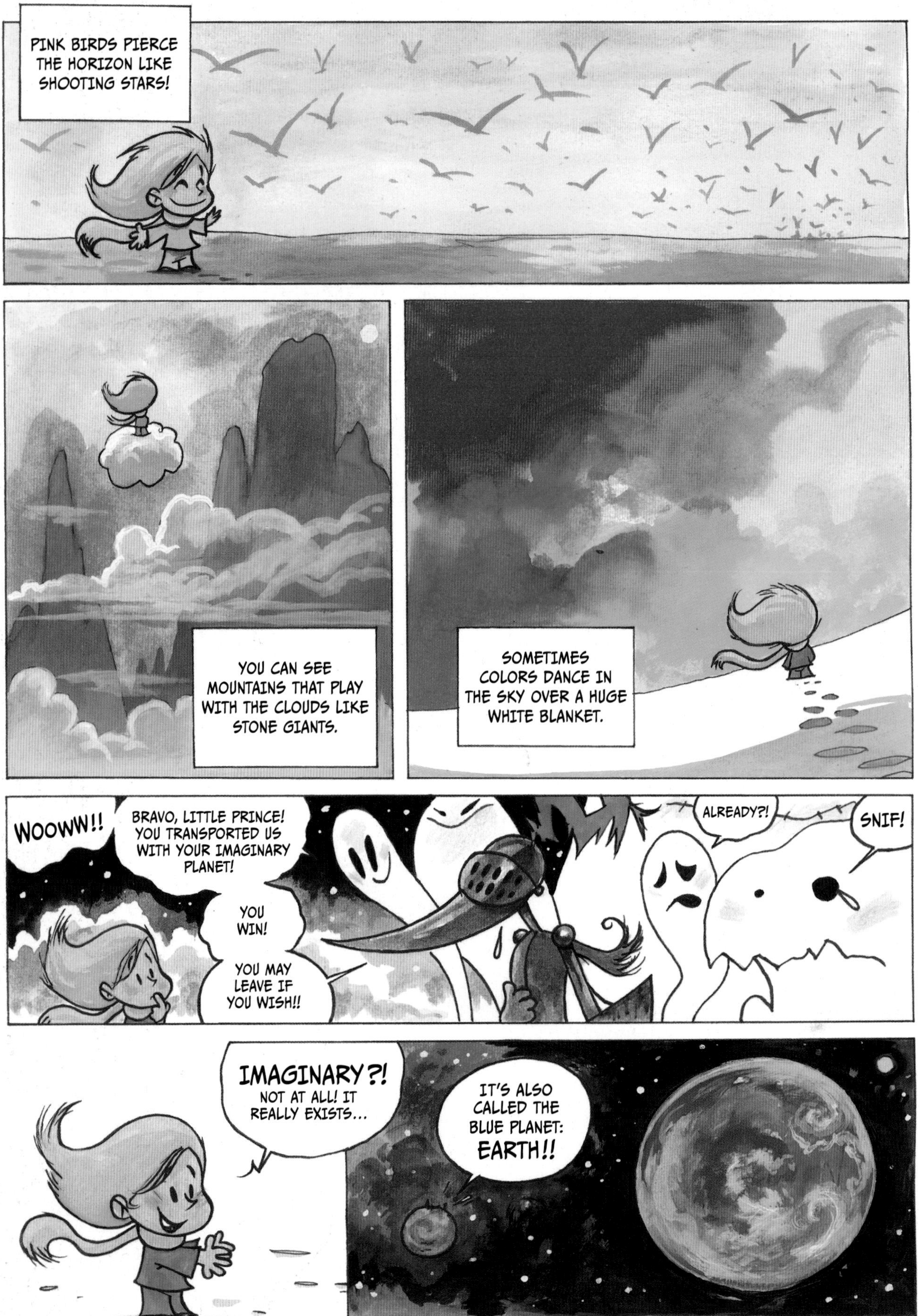
PINK BIRDS PIERCE THE HORIZON LIKE SHOOTING STARS!
YOU CAN SEE MOUNTAINS THAT PLAY WITH THE CLOUDS LIKE STONE GIANTS.
SOMETIMES COLORS DANCE IN THE SKY OVER A HUGE WHITE BLANKET.
WOOWW!!
BRAVO, LITTLE PRINCE! YOU TRANSPORTED US WITH YOUR IMAGINARY PLANET!
YOU WIN!
YOU MAY LEAVE IF YOU WISH!!
ALREADY?!
SNIF!
IMAGINARY?! NOT AT ALL! IT REALLY EXISTS...
IT'S ALSO CALLED THE BLUE PLANET: EARTH!!

TRANSLATION BY CAROL BURRELL
WITH EXTRA PUNS DREAMED UP BY ANNE AND OWEN SMITH

ANTOINE DE SAINT-EXUPÉRY
Aviator • Author • Adventurer • Hero

Antoine de Saint-Exupéry, author of the novel *The Little Prince* on which these new adventures are based, was born on June 29, 1900, in Lyon, France. He was the third of five children: Marie-Madeleine, Simone, Antoine, François, and Gabrielle. It was when he was twelve years old, during his summer break from boarding school, that airplanes and flying first made a huge impression on him.

In 1920, he was accepted into the École des Beaux-Arts in Paris to study architecture, but the next year he joined the Second Aviation Regiment of the armed forces and received his pilot's license. In 1922, he had his first plane crash and suffered a head fracture. He had to leave the armed forces and work at different jobs on the ground to earn a living.

By May of 1926, Saint-Exupéry was able to fly again. He delivered airmail, which was a new and sometimes dangerous profession, on routes from France to Senegal and all the way to South America. That was where, in 1931, he met and married Consuelo Suncin.

From 1933 to 1938, Saint-Exupéry was very busy. He traveled to North Africa and Indochina and attempted to break the flight speed record from Paris to Saigon, Vietnam—during which his plane crashed again. It went down in the middle of the Sahara Desert. After his recovery, his life became even busier. He wrote newspaper reports in Spain on the Spanish Civil War, scouted airplane routes between Casablanca and Timbuktu, wrote a screenplay, registered several patents, and traveled to the United States. In 1939, with the start of World War II, he returned to France and talked his way into a job as a high-risk reconnaissance pilot for the French Air Force. But this only lasted until France reached an armistice agreement with Germany.

In December 1940, Saint-Exupéry returned to visit friends in New York, where he finally began work on *The Little Prince.* The story is narrated by a pilot who has crashed his plane into the Sahara Desert. He meets a little prince visiting from a faraway asteroid. Along the way, the prince also meets Fox and Snake. By late 1942, after spending the spring and summer writing and illustrating, Saint-Exupéry had completed his novel, and in April 1943 it was published in his native language of French *(Le Petit Prince)* and in English.

Saint-Exupéry was eager to return to the war. He decided to join the Free French Forces in Algeria, who were continuing the fight against the Axis powers. Because of his age, at first he had a hard time convincing them to let him fly. He was authorized to fly five dangerous missions. In fact, he flew eight. On July 31, 1944, Saint-Exupéry went on a scouting flight to prepare for military landings in the south of France. His plane disappeared over the water, and he was never seen again.

Over the decades since *The Little Prince* was published, it has gone on to become one of the best-selling novels of all time. In 2003, a small moon in our solar system's asteroid belt was named Petit-Prince in honor of the masterpiece Saint-Exupéry created.

and poetic sensibility. Sixty-five years after the first edition, the Saint-Exupéry Estate decided to bring the character back for a whole new generation . . . and for everyone who has ever loved the boy who sees the world with his heart.

The Little Prince now returns in a series of new adventures that remain true to the spirit of the original work. He will travel from planet to planet chasing the wicked Snake, who wants to plunge the whole universe into darkness. On each planet, the Snake sends bad thoughts into the minds of its inhabitants, making them sad and grim, draining the life out of their planet. The Little Prince must leave his beautiful Rose behind and must use his vision and courage to defeat the Snake, bringing along his friend Fox to save planets in danger across the universe.

ABOUT THE ADAPTERS

After several years in video games and Japanese animation, adapter Guillaume Dorison became literary editor for the publisher Les Humanoïdes Associés in 2006, where he launched the Shogun Collection dedicated to original manga. In June 2010, he founded Élyum Studio with Didier Poli, Jean-Baptiste Hostache, and Xavier Dorison to provide services for the creation of graphic novels. In addition to his position as director of writing for Élyum Studio, he has more than two dozen comics and manga to his credit under the pseudonym IZU, has written several titles in the Explora series on world explorers for French publisher Glénat, and won the 2010 Animeland Prize for best French manga.

Didier Poli, artistic director for the new graphic novel adaptations based on *The Little Prince*, was born in Lyon in 1971. After graduate studies in applied arts, he worked for various animation studios including Disney. He was working as artistic director for the video game company Kalisto Entertainment when he met Manuel Bichebois in 2001 and began drawing Bichebois's graphic novel series L'Enfant de l'orage. At the 2004 Nîmes Festival, Didier Poli received the Bronze Boar prize for young talent. He continues, along with his work on graphic novels, to work regularly in cartoons and video games as a designer and storyboard artist.